Dear Bruce Springsteen

A Novel

Kevin Major

Published by
Dell Publishing
a division of
Bantam Doubleday Dell Publishing Group, Inc.
666 Fifth Avenue
New York, New York 10103

ISBN: 0-440-20410-0

RL: 4.2

Reprinted by arrangement with Delacorte Press

Printed in the United States of America

July 1989

10 9 8 7 6 5 4 3 2 1

KRI

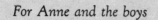

For Anne and the boys

Dear Bruce Springsteen,

This letter might never get to you. If it does, it might take years before you get around to reading it because you must get tons of mail. I'm going to write it anyway.

You see, I just want to say how much I like your music and to tell you a bit about myself. I don't want to take up much of your time. You probably got millions of things on your mind, but I figure if you ever had a few spare minutes you wouldn't mind listening. That's the kind of person I figure you are.

My name is Terry Blanchard. The story goes that my father named me after a buddy of his from high school who was killed in a motorcycle accident. I heard someone say once that the old man was going to go riding with him that day but changed his mind at the last minute. It's just what I've heard. He never really talked about it.

Hey, know what I just figured out? That you're old enough to be my father. In fact, my old man and you must be about the same age. Weird, right? You're not that much alike though.

I'm getting off track. I'm fourteen. I'm in the ninth grade at school. I got a sister who's ten. The place where I live is not very big, fifteen thousand people maybe. Big enough to have a McDonald's and a few other things, if that means anything. There are a lot worse places to live, I guess. It used to be better, when the mill wasn't getting rid of people.

Bored yet? Guess I shouldn't be taking up your time.

Anyway, I just want to say that I really get off on your music and that my biggest dream is to see you in concert someday. Man, from the clips I've seen on TV, the concerts must be wicked.

Yours truly,
Terry

Dear Bruce Springsteen,

I wrote you about a week and a half ago. Maybe you never got the letter. (The only address I could find is the address of the record company I got off the back of one of your albums.) I hope they sent the letter on to you. If they didn't, it don't make much difference. I didn't say much. And I don't really figure on getting an answer.

So why am I at this again?

Who knows? I guess because I feel like it. I read over again one of the stories about you from *Rolling Stone*. See, I think I probably got some of the same feelings in my guts you had when you were my age. And there's nobody I really feel like talking to.

Ever wake up in the morning and think, hell, I'd rather stay in bed than have to get up and face another day in school? You must've. After reading that story about how your third-grade teacher rammed you down a garbage can at school, I guess you did. Some of my teachers are real winners, too. They'd never go so far as to stuff someone down a garbage can, but they do things that make you feel just as bad. Like today when Jenkins, the math teacher I got, told me I got a brain that's permanently unemployed, and that's what the rest of me is going to be if I don't do some work. I felt like telling him right off, but of course I didn't. Anyway, the guy's weird. We call him Jerkins. He thinks he's real macho. He's like six feet two, with a beer gut that he tries to keep sucked in, and he wears three or four gold chains with eagles and rams' heads and stuff like that on them. Man, the guy's got real problems.

Then there's Mrs. Lamb. She's like something out of the Dark Ages. She should retire and give the world a break. She's got no time for any of the guys in the class except for the ones who get A's all the time. I gave up trying to get her to help me during English class because every time, she figures she's got to lecture me about not paying attention when she explained it the first time.

See, one thing that really got me into your music was this line in "No Surrender," the line about busting out of class. I really feel like that a lot of times. I'd never do it because for one thing my mother would have my neck. And when I think about it long enough, I got to admit I have got a few half-decent teachers. There's actually one or two I get along with most of the time. But you know the way it is. Some teachers can really grind you the wrong way.

After I started listening to the lyrics in that song, they got to mean a lot to me. Especially the parts about having dreams. No retreat, and no surrender. Right?

Up to then, all I was doing was liking the music and not paying much attention to what the songs were about. Now I got copies of all the lyrics to all your songs. I got a full set of tapes, right back to *Greetings from Asbury Park*. (It's hard to get that one around here. I had my cousin pick it up for me Christmas when he was in Florida.)

Guess I should call it quits now. If this letter ever gets to you, then I don't want to hog your time. By the way, you know, if you get this letter and want me to stop writing, just tell me and I won't bug you again.

Take it easy,
Terry (Blanchard)

P.S. "Yours truly" is what Lamb tells us to use. What does she know? I'm trying to be different.

Dear Bruce Springsteen,

I never got an answer to either one of my letters, so I guess that means you don't mind me writing.

That's a little joke. I heard you're on tour in Japan. My letters are probably at the bottom of a sack of fan mail in your record company's basement somewhere.

I can handle that. I'm writing to you anyway because I like doing it, that's all. Even if they're not getting to you, yet.

Today in school Jerkins was on my back again. Man, if he don't quit picking on me, one of these days he's going to get more than he bargained for. I was tapping my fingers on the desk to some music that was running around in my head. First he used his regular put-down: "Empty vessels make the most noise." I don't know where the hell he got that from. He uses it so often, you'd think he'd get sick of it. I sure am. Then he said, "Blanchard, smarten up. We all know how easy it is for you to make a fool of yourself. You don't have to keep proving it."

I never said nothing back to him. Not that I didn't have a few things in my mind. What I thought about doing was roping him to his chair, then plunking a ghetto blaster on the desk in front of him and vibrating his eardrums with one of your songs, one of the real rockers like "Cadillac Ranch" or "Ramrod." Just to teach him a few things about what's noise and what's not. You picture that? I could, for the whole rest of math class. My imagination I figure is what gets me through the day half the time.

It's got to be great to let loose like you do onstage. To rip into a song with all you got and have everything what's inside you come out. And not have to answer to anybody for it. The most I do is slam a few doors. That really don't do the job.

A few times when there's been nobody in the house, only me, I've cranked up one of your songs on eight or nine and made out I was singing it, with a flashlight or something for a mike. Once, Mrs. MacKinnon from next door showed up·in the apartment and caught me. Man, talk about turn red. I probably glowed. She had no reason to be nosing around. She said the music was so loud, she thought something was wrong. Likely story. Of course she had to tell my mother, although Mom never said much. Now I use headphones, but it's not the same. You can't really cut loose.

I got my eyes on a poster of you in concert right now. Man, the sweat is just pourin' off you, but it looks like you're having a wicked time. That's the only poster I got on my bedroom wall anymore. My kid sister's got some pictures of you on her wall that she cut from some of those stupid magazines she buys. It looks dumb because she's got you next to this bunch of wimps dressed in sparkly clothes. She don't know any better. Man, she don't know you're The Boss. When she starts talking about you I got to leave the room. It's so dumb, it's embarrassing. She's dumb about a lot of things, if you really want to know.

It's about midnight, and everyone's gone to bed long ago. I better turn off the light and try to get some sleep. Can't wait for tomorrow. Another wonderful week of school. Thank God there's only two months left before the summer break.

Cutting loose,
Terry (Blanchard)

Dear Bruce Springsteen,

Remember me?

How was Japan? I heard about your concerts there on the FM rock station I listen to. It must have been wild.

Maybe you'd like to know a bit about my family. (Then again, maybe you wouldn't. But I'm warning you, you might get material for a good song out of this.)

My mother is okay. I mean, we get along okay most of the time. We have our days, but most times she's pretty decent. She cares a lot about me, and I figure that's got to mean a lot. I'll give you an example. The other day when she got home from work and was looking like she had a hell of a day at the hospital (and besides, she was coming down with a cold), she went through all the trouble of making spaghetti with real spaghetti sauce because she knows I can't handle the stuff from a bottle. I helped her, but she did most of the work. I told her to go lie down for a while, but she wouldn't have any of that. I know part of it is she don't want to have anyone say she can't take care of us the same as if she weren't doing shift work all the time.

She's a nursing assistant. She likes her job, but it's hard work. She's on her feet a lot. I get the inside track on all the accidents and who's having what baby and all that, so there's lots to talk about sometimes. Some of it she'll only tell me after Amanda's gone to bed. That's the best of it — the two of us in the kitchen, drinking coffee and talking about stuff like that. Some of what goes on in a hospital you wouldn't believe.

She used to work just part-time. It's only been the past few months that she's been able to get on full-time. She don't like the shift work much, but she got no choice. She keeps saying she's lucky to have a job at all. We need the money. It's either that or welfare again. She says that every so often like she needs to keep the record straight. I guess she feels guilty that we haven't got it so good as a lot of other people, that she can't give us some of the things that she'd like to. She keeps saying we could have it a lot worse. We could be starving to death in Africa. Or be like the Smiths down the street.

The Smiths are this family who moved into one of the apartments not far from us after their house burned down. A baby-sitter was making french fries on the stove late in the night and then fell asleep watching TV. The fat caught fire. Lucky the smoke woke her up and she got the kids out in time. It's pretty sad because they never had insurance and now they got nothing.

I know things could be a lot worse for us. I just wish Mom wouldn't keep bringing it up. I can look at the news on TV and see for myself that we got it better than lots of people in the world.

Did you ever think about how you came to be born where you did? Whether or not it was just chance. Like, if you added up all the kids that was born on any one day, the chances are probably half a million to one that you'd end up being born where you did. It was a darn sight more likely that you would have popped out in some country halfway around the world, next to a mudhole someplace. And probably not know a stupid thing about rock music or hamburgers or stuff like that. Man, I know it's a crazy way to look at things, but I've thought a lot about that. I guess we have got it better than running around with no clothes on wondering where the next meal is coming from. Whenever I get real fed up with things, that sort of sticks in my mind.

Amanda don't see it that way. She gives Mom a hard time sometimes because she asks for stuff that she should know we can't afford. Then when she has got money, instead of saving it for something she really needs, she'll blow it all on junk like those dumb magazines she buys. (No offense, it's not your picture she buys them for, it's Duran Duran). Last Christmas Mom went through hell to get a certain type of doll. (Freckles, brown hair, and blue eyes — do you believe it?) And now she hardly ever plays with it. She says it's too childish. She's heavy into makeup these days. I never said anything to Mom, but I know Amanda gets into her eyeliner and crap like that when Mom is at work some evenings. She disappears for an hour and comes back looking like a half-size Madonna. Man, it drives me crazy the way she flits around sometimes.

I got to go. There's a Tom Cruise movie on TV. Movies are what I like best on TV next to the late-night video shows.

Signing off for now,
Terry

Dear Bruce Springsteen,

Me again. I'm getting off on this. I never thought I'd have much to talk about. I don't care if the letters pile up and pile up and never get to you for months.

It's getting to be almost like a diary. Jerkins once called something I wrote "verbal diarrhea." Man, don't believe it. He thought he was being real smart, the overgrown dummy.

I should get to the reason I wanted to write to you in the first place. I've been putting it off.

You're probably wondering where my old man's been all this time. I haven't been talking about him. He's been gone for about six months now — gone off somewhere. I got an idea where, but I don't know for sure. Mom might know, but I don't think she does. I'm not sure anymore if she really cares.

Things were getting pretty touchy between them for a long time before that. Actually, for as long as I can remember, they used to argue. Sometimes it wasn't so nice, although it never got to be more than words. For the month or so before he took off, it started getting worse. Till one day I came home from school and Mom said he was gone. I figured she just meant for a few days to look for work or something, but what she really meant was that he packed up and took off for good. I didn't know what to say.

I thought maybe when things cooled down and each of them started thinking about it, they'd try getting back together. It never happened.

She never did come out and say why he ran off like he did. I got a pretty good idea, but I'm not saying nothing to Mom. I figure he had someone else he was going out with—another woman. I wish it wasn't true, but I'm pretty sure it is. And I got a feeling I might know where to find him. Dad knows the owner of this club in Callum called BJ's. The guy booked the band in there once. Just for a favor, because they have mostly rock bands play there. I overheard Dad on the phone talking to the guy after they got back, and before he hung up he asked about this person Charlene.

I forgot to tell you that he played in a band. Actually, I didn't forget. I was saving it for the right moment. It wasn't a rock band. They played some rock, but they played mostly country music, because that's the only thing that goes over any good in most of the clubs around here. As it was, there was only ever enough work for weekends. Sometimes not that. They played a lot of Waylon Jennings and George Jones, Ricky Scaggs, stuff like that. Now and then they'd throw in a little rock, depending on the crowd. I even heard them play "Cadillac Ranch" at a practice once. They crucified it. You would have been grinding your teeth for a week. I can't listen to that song anymore without thinking about that.

I know he would have liked to have been at it all the time, but there just wasn't the work to keep a four-man band going full-time. If there was more money around, maybe. With so much unemployment, clubs just can't afford to hire bands during the week. If they'd tried making it in some place bigger, then maybe they could have made a go of it. But Nev and

Brian, they were both hanging on to jobs with a construction company over in White Falls, and they weren't about to give that up. Anyway, I don't think the band was good enough. Even the old man gave up talking like they were after a while.

Besides the band, he used to get other jobs when he could. He worked in the maintenance shop for the heavy equipment before they started laying off people at the mill. After that he was usually lucky enough to get a few weeks here and a few weeks there, so's he'd qualify for his unemployment insurance before the winter came. Only a couple of times did we have to go on welfare. Just before he took off was one of them.

Mom was pretty fed up, having to live that way — not knowing from one month to the next how much money we'd have. Dad blamed it on the government, said they didn't give a damn about us around here. Mom was always after him to move away again, go back out West where we used to live. He didn't want to. He said this was where he was born and he liked it here and it was the government's job to see that the place didn't just die off and be forgotten about.

I guess he's right. I guess it don't make much difference anymore, now that he's gone. He couldn't have liked it that much, or he wouldn't have taken off like he done.

What do I think of him going? Sure it still bugs me. I can't say we were ever really close. We never did spend enough time together. Still, you know, he is my father. And with him around, there was at least a chance of things getting better between us.

I don't know. I think about it a lot. I hope he does come back. I'm counting on it.

Sorry I went on for so long.

I better go. See ya,
Terry

Dear Bruce Springsteen,

I know I got no real right to dump all this personal stuff on you. I thought about it yesterday after I sent the last letter. Here I am, probably making a fool of myself, going on and on about my life to someone I never even met.

Then when I thought about it some more, I felt like I almost know you. I've read everything I can lay my hands on that's been written about you. I've gone to the library and dug out old copies of *Rolling Stone* from six and seven years ago. I've read three full-length books on you, three times each. I play your music all the time. (Man, my ghetto blaster practically spits back any tape that's not yours.)

And in a way you're sort of a connection between me and my father. For my fourteenth birthday he gave me one of your tapes. Then a week after that he was gone.

It was the first time he ever went out of his way to give me a present himself. Usually it was something from the both of them. I can hear him now when he handed it to me: "It's about time you got over that heavy-metal crap. Listen to something decent for a change." He gave me the tape, and he never said nothing else about it.

I knew he was into your music a lot. He never listened to it much in the house, mostly when he was driving the old van we used to have. Mostly then by himself. The four of us were in the van once and he put on *Nebraska*. Mom made him take it off because, she said, it sounded too depressing. He sort of grunted something about she didn't know what good music was and popped out the tape. She said if you're going to spend money we can't afford on music, then you might as well spend it on something that'll cheer you up. He ignored her.

After that he never played your music much when Mom was around. But I know the tapes must have been used a lot. He had a special place in the van where he kept them. Once when it was just the two of us driving someplace to pick up some secondhand furniture, he put on *The River*. The only song of yours I knew from that tape was "Hungry Heart." Everything was sort of quiet between us, so I said to him that I liked that song. He said he liked it, too, he liked the words.

I never thought about that much till after he left. Then I bought the tape and started paying attention to the words. The old man's got a hungry heart.

So now you know some of the reason why I'm writing these crazy letters. There's more to it than that. I got dreams about things I want to do when I get older.

Dream on, right?
Terry

Dear Bruce Springsteen,

I got something new to tell you. Remember what I said about getting along with Mom? Well, you can forget it.

She's been pestering me and pestering me for months now to get my math marks up so I'd at least have a chance of passing math at the end of the year. I can't get through ninth grade without it.

She said, "I know you can do it. All you have to do is get it in your head that you're going to try. You only need fifty percent to pass."

She's right. I know I could pass if I worked at it. I just haven't got no interest in it, especially with that Jerkins for a teacher.

"I'll make you a deal," I said.

"Go ahead."

"I'll pass math. And when we can afford it, you loan me fifty bucks."

She grinned, like she figured I was joking. "What for?"

"With what I got saved, I can buy a secondhand electric guitar and amp."

She never said anything right away. But I could tell by the look she gave me that it wasn't something she wanted to hear. "Surely to God you can find a better use for money than that."

"I'm not askin' you to give me any. Only a loan."

"No way. It'll only be a waste. You can't play."

"I can learn. I been playing around with that old acoustic belonging to Dad."

"I know that."

"Well?"

"Well, don't you think I haven't had enough of that? Your father wasted his life thinking he could make a living playing in a band."

"Who said anything about a band?"

"I did. And you will be, too, before long."

"All right, all right. Forget it. I don't want your money. I'll get it myself somewhere."

I got up from the table and headed for my room.

"Terry, listen to me," she said, trying to sound fair about it all now, when it was too late. I went into the room and slammed the door.

Before long she came knocking at it.

I didn't answer her.

She opened the door real slow and looked in. "If it was anything else —"

"I said I don't want your lousy money."

"Terry, you're not trying to see my point of view."

"You're not trying to see mine."

"You know what your father was like!" she yelled. "What kind of life do you think it's been for me?" She realized she was yelling and stopped. Then she said, "What about me? You think it's fair? Just ask yourself that."

"You married him."

"Yeah, so you could have a father."

I just stared at her. It took a long time with neither one of us saying anything, before it sunk in what she'd said.

She came in the room and stood at the end of the bed. "I'm sorry. I didn't mean for it to come out like that."

"So that's the reason you married him."

"No, that's not the reason. We loved each other then. Enough to get married."

I think she would have said something else if I never got up and walked out of the room. I grabbed my jacket from the hall closet and took off outdoors.

That ended that.

I'm thinking now I should have got a few things straight. Like, what does she think of him now? Don't she ever want him to come back again?

I was mad. More at myself than anybody, for being so stupid not to have that figured out before now. It never crossed my mind. It should've.

Not that it changes much. She's still my mother, and he's still my father. I just don't understand why they stuck together as long as they did. Somebody answer me that.

This is a hell of a way to end a letter.

Man, you're getting more than you bargained for if you bothered to read about this mess.

Terry

Dear Bruce Springsteen,

Guess what I got on the math test I got back today? 71. I'm not telling Mom and I'm not going to mention money to her again. I guess I studied out of spite. When Jerkins handed back the test, he gave me a dirty look, like he figured I cheated. Lucky for him he never said anything.

Me and Mom have been pretty edgy with each other since that blowup a while back. She's been trying to get on the good side of me with little remarks that are supposed to cheer me up. I've been trying to make it look like what she said don't bother me anymore.

I been practicing a lot with the guitar. It's not in too good a shape. I don't think the old man could have paid much for it when he bought it, and that must have been twenty years ago.

I been staying in after school, two afternoons a week, to sit in on Kirkland's guitar class. He's the music teacher, and he's been having special classes for anyone interested in playing guitar. I learned a lot so far. He says I got potential. Sounds good to me.

I been fooling around a lot at home, too. And a couple of times I've gone over to Sean's house, and we've worked out a few tunes together. Sean is this guy I got to know from going to Kirkland's classes. I knew him a bit before (he was in my homeroom last year), but now we've started to hang around together. He's pretty decent. It don't bother him that other people probably think I'm weird. Actually, there's not much that does bother him. He jokes around and carries on a lot. I wish sometimes I could be more like that.

Anyway, we've sort of hit it off okay. He's got a real nice Yamaha guitar. (His old man owns a furniture business, and I'd say they got a few bucks.) Last night before we went to the movie, we were working on "Dancing in the Dark." He likes your music. He's not nuts about it like I am, which is all right, because I get off on the fact that I know things about you that nobody else does.

We went to see a real blood-and-guts movie last night. Everybody I heard talk about it after really liked it. They thought it was great seeing people getting their brains blowed out and twelve-inch blades rammed into their guts. I didn't get off on it myself. To me the whole thing wasn't very real. Sean said afterward that it was only a movie, nobody is suppose to think it could really happen that way. Maybe he's right, maybe I do think about things too much. But that's just the way I am.

Know something? It's got to the point where I don't really care anymore if what I think of something is different from what everybody else thinks. I know I don't fit in so hot most of the time, but like I said to Sean, I'm used to spending a lot of time alone. I've spent hours just lying around down by the river listening to tapes, just thinking about things I'd like to do someday. One thing I really want to do is travel around a lot, find out what things are like in other places.

Know something else? Mom is right. I would like to try playing in a band. I think I'll soon have Sean sold on the idea, too. I keep bringing it up every chance I get. He's not so sure we could pull it off, but give me a while longer and I'll have him convinced. I haven't got a clue who else we could get or how good we'd be. But you never know till you try, right? That's the way I got it figured.

By the way, we watched *The Buddy Holly Story* the other night, on the VCR over at Sean's place. I've been dying to see it ever since I read about how much you liked it. It was great. If you want to make it, you got to start off believing in yourself, right? Now there's a movie that was real.

Rave on,
Terry

Dear Bruce Springsteen,

I decided to hell with it. Man, there's only so much I can take from that jerk.

It all started the other day when I wore a headband to school. It was only a piece of denim I cut from the sleeve of my old jean jacket. I got a few weird looks, which I expected because the guys at the school I go to are superstraight when it comes to how they dress. Anything different, and they look at you like you got seven heads. I can handle that.

But in math class Jerkins said to me, "Need something to keep your brains from leaking out?" I didn't pay no attention to him.

"Come on, get that silly thing off your head."

When I still ignored him he went right snaky, saying I had to take it off because it was headgear and there's a rule in the school about wearing anything like that in class. I told you the guy's got problems.

"It's not headgear," I said. "It's on my forehead, not on the top of my head."

"I told you to get it off. You're distracting the other students."

Can you believe this guy? I knew why he was doing it. He's got it in for me, and he won't be satisfied till he sees me suffer. He still thinks I cheated on that math test.

"Laura's got something on *her* head. You didn't ask her to take *that* off." Laura sits up front in the row next to me. She's always wearing some crazy getup. She had a hairband on with a hot pink something or other coming out of it. I wasn't sure I was doing the right thing, because comparing myself to a girl was like asking for trouble.

Sure enough, Jerkins fires back with, "That's different. Wear one of those if you want. I'm sure Laura wouldn't mind lending you hers. You'd really look cute."

The class broke up laughing. And he looked at me with this dirty smirk on his face.

"Take it off, or get out of my class."

Up yours, man, I said just to myself.

But I kept my cool. I stood up by my desk. "I'd like to see the rule where it says I can't wear one," I told him, real calm.

"Don't play smart with me, Blanchard."

"Then I'll go to the principal and check it out for myself." I knew I had to be careful not to lose my temper and blow it.

That really got to him. You could see the blood rise up in his face.

"I make the rules in this class!" He headed toward me. "Sit down!" he yelled.

"You just told me to get out."

"Sit down before I sit you down!"

He made a move with his hand toward my head.

"I wouldn't touch that if I were you," I said, glaring at him.

His hand stopped. He tried to force that same dirty smirk onto his face. But it wasn't quite the same.

He looked at me a while longer, then walked up the aisle and out the classroom door without saying another word.

I sat down in my seat again. But nobody else moved a muscle. There were a few chuckles from the back of the class.

After a couple of minutes Jerkins came back in and sat at his desk.

"Get to work," he said. He didn't look directly at anyone, just kept his eyes moving around the class. "And don't let me hear one sound from anybody."

After about a minute he looked down at me. "Blanchard, you can keep that thing on your head for now. You might need it for a bandage before the year is over."

A few people laughed. Not many.

Man, I knew I'd got him good.

I don't know if he went to the principal or not. All I know is, he's never said a word about the headband since. And I've worn it to school every single day.

I can't wait till tomorrow to see what he'll say about what I got done with my hair. I got it cut short, and then I dyed it a lighter color, almost blond. I think it looks great — makes me look different, anyway. I been thinking about it for weeks, and this little incident with the headband got me so dirty that I went ahead and did it.

I mixed up a mess of peroxide and lemon juice and mineral oil. I washed my hair, then dumped that stuff on and went out in the sun. When it dried out it was a bit lighter, but not light enough. By that time it was clouded over outside. I dumped the stuff on a couple of more times and give it to 'er with the hair dryer. It worked.

It takes a bit of getting used to. I got to look at myself twice in the mirror every time I go to the can. I think it suits me. My hair was never real dark anyway, just a dirty brown color. Now it's dirty blond.

Sean dropped by, and when he saw my hair he busted out laughing. He said I looked really freaked out. I handed him what was left of the stuff I had mixed up. He made out he was thinking about it. Go for it, I told him, and I stood there and waited. But no way. I know why, even though he wouldn't admit it. He was afraid his parents would throw a fit.

Not me. When Mom came home she just about had a bird. "And you call Amanda crazy!" she said. I don't care.

Stay cool,
Terry

Dear Bruce Springsteen,

Jerkins didn't recognize me at first. And when he finally figured out it was me, he didn't know what to do. Like the wires in his head had screwed up.

He never said much except "Now we'll know if blondes have more fun," whatever that's supposed to mean. There's not much he could say. There was no rule he could fake for this one. I was kind of hoping he would say something. I would have taken it right straight to the principal.

Man, I wish you could have seen his face, though. It was like he just took a whiff of rotten garbage. When class was over I grinned at him as I was going out the door. Just to rub it in a bit. He hates me even more now.

Lovin' it,
Terry

Dear Bruce Springsteen,

You know, some people look at me, and just because I don't go around like one of them, they think my brain cells are rotting or something. They take me for someone who's pretty dumb.

I think I must have a lot of stuff on my mind that nobody else does. I'll pass people on the street, and they'll look at me like I'm something extinct. I'll sort of smile if I notice them, and half the time they'll go by me like they haven't even seen me. Except now they sometimes laugh because of my hair.

I can handle it. I used to worry that they figured I must really be weird. Like I said before, now I don't care much what they think.

I still spend a lot of time in my room, by myself. My room is not the tidiest. Mom is always after me to clean it up. There's an old black and white TV that don't work anymore, that I took apart to have a look at but can't fix. There's junk around that I've had since I was nine or ten, like models of cars and vans and stuff with parts that have come unglued. I should clear that junk out, but I never seem to get around to doing it. Like the Pepsi bottle on the dresser with the neck melted and hauled out of shape. I won that at a fair one summer when we were on vacation.

The room is not very big. There's hardly space enough for the bed and the dresser, let alone the rest of the junk. The only half-decent spot is where I keep my ghetto blaster and tapes. I got it right up next to the bed and near the window so the antenna wire will reach outdoors. It picks up FM pretty good, especially in the nighttime. That's when they play the best music, anyway.

I spend a lot of time in there listening to music, mostly with headphones. That's the way I do my homework. Sometimes I just lie there with the headphones on and fool around with the set of handgrips I got or something. There's a few guitar magazines in there, and Rolling Stone. I get them cheap at the used bookstore. And there's a few paperbacks.

The window in my room looks out on a parking lot. Not what you'd call exciting. Except one night last week these guys in a Camaro parked there really late and in the darkest corner of the lot. I'm sure they came there to smoke up. After an hour or so they peeled out with the windows down and laughing their heads off. Maybe they had girls with them. Maybe it wasn't just dope they were playing around with.

Girls is one thing I think a lot about. Although I can't say it's the main thing. A few of the fellows in my classes got girl friends, but I'm not into that. I figure I got lots of time yet. Besides, I wouldn't have the guts to ask a girl to go out with me. If I go to a school dance I usually hang around the canteen a lot or sit somewhere and listen to the music. Now and then a girl might ask me to dance. It's not the most popular ones who do it, but then again, who am I to complain? I'm not exactly your five-star teenage idol.

There's one or two girls I got my eye on. One named Joanne who's really nice. But that's about as far as it goes — my eye. I could if I wanted to, you know, force myself to ask a girl out. It would probably mean a nervous breakdown, but I probably could do it if I really wanted to. I figure it's not worth the trouble. That don't stop me from thinking about it, thinking about all the things I would do if I wasn't so slow around girls. I'll get over it someday. (Don't hold your breath.) I remember reading about the trouble you had with girls when you were my age. And look at you now, you're married. Something must have changed.

Sean hasn't got a girl friend, either, although that's half he talks about — getting one. There's two or three girls who really like him and call him up all the time. I haven't got that problem. Except for Amanda talking, our phone is like dead silence most of the time.

Sean says, "Man, it's wicked. Some girls, they're real great to talk to. Others, they'll stay on the line forever if I didn't give them some crap line about having to go do my homework or something."

Probably I don't know how good I got it.

Hanging up for now,
Terry

P.S. I guess I do know how good I got it in other ways. I went to the convenience store at the end of the street to get some milk just before I started this letter. Some of the Smiths (the ones who had the fire) were ahead of me at the checkout. Mrs. Smith had an armload of groceries, and when she went to pay for them she was something like fifty cents short, and she had to put one of the things back. I really felt sorry for her. You could tell just by the way they looked that the family must be having a real rough time of it.

Dear Bruce Springsteen,

Quick update on the girl situation.

This girl comes up to me in the hall at school this morning and says, "I like your hair. Hang in there. You got guts." Right out of nowhere. Then she strolls on up the hall.

I got such a surprise, my jaw probably dropped ten feet or something. I turned red, of course. I never had time to say anything. Not that anything very brilliant would have come out. What could I say? I still haven't figured that out.

Anyway, that's not the end of it. Tonight this same girl calls me up. I knew right away it was her. She didn't have to tell me her name, but she did anyway — Kristy. She made a point of telling me it's spelled with a K. She said she just wanted to call me up to say she was sorry if she embarrassed me in the hall this morning, but that she really did think it was great what I did to myself. I stammered and stuttered like I had a bagful of cottonballs in my mouth. Man, I must have sounded like a real idiot. Then she said she's got to go but would I like to meet her sometime, like for a burger or something, her treat?

I said, "No, that's all right. I mean, sure I would. But I can pay. But if you want to, really, then I don't mind, okay?"

Get the picture? I screwed it up, real sweet. I couldn't have done a better job on myself if I had swallowed the receiver.

After she hung up I could have booted myself a hundred times for sounding so stupid. Then I figured it out perfect what I should have said.

Now what do I do? What I should do is call her up and try sounding like I got a brain. That's what I should do, but I won't. I haven't got the guts. Not tonight. Maybe tomorrow night. But then it might be too late. She's probably got all these weird thoughts crawling around in her head about what a turd I am that I can't even carry on a sensible conversation over the phone. Maybe if I do call her up I'll screw it up again, and then she'll think for sure I'm in need of repair.

> I'll sleep on it.
> Terry

P.S. (*an hour later*) The trouble is I can't sleep on it. I can't get to sleep. Period.

Dear Bruce Springsteen,

I'm writing this in math class. We got a substitute instead of Jerkins, and it's supposed to be a study period.

I saw Kristy in school again today. She passed me in the hall and never said nothing, but she was almost smiling. I was, too. I hope she noticed.

I got to call her up. It's the only way I'm going to get to talk to her alone. If I try anything at school, I'll never know who might show up. And if someone else is around, I might as well pack it in because I'll never get two words straight.

I'll do it tonight. I swear I will. If I don't, I promise to God I'll write the next letter in blood, my own.

The substitute is giving me weird looks. I better stop writing before she gets it in her head to come this way. If she gets a look at this letter, I'll be in real you-know-what.

Six hours later:
No blood. No phone call yet, but no blood.
I called, but the line was busy.
After an hour working up to it, too. I had the first six digits dialed about a dozen different times. I never got to the last

one. Then Amanda started banging at the door to get in. (I had the phone strung into the bathroom with the door closed.) I had to come out and let her use the can and then start the torture all over again. That's just what it was—torture, pure and simple. Even though I had it written down on a piece of paper what I wanted to say.

Finally, I couldn't handle it anymore. I said to hell with it and dialed the last digit. My heart was pounding. (I haven't sweated that much since we did the mile run in gym class.) Then nothing but a busy signal. I was relieved in one way, but now I got to go through all that again.

Writing this letter is a little break, something to do with my hands. I'm going crazy. The pressure is getting to me.

In one way I don't care if I do call. So what if she never speaks to me again? Then, I'm thinking, I do care. It's the first time a girl's ever paid much attention to me. I should be taking advantage of it. Even if she never says a word to me again, at least I should set her straight on what I'm really like. At least she should know what she's missing.

An hour later:

I did it. I talked to her on the phone. For almost ten minutes. Well, seven or eight minutes. I timed it. Not that it did me much good, though.

Her father answered the phone.

"Could I speak to Kristy, please?"

"Kristy, it's for you again."

Right away I started thinking she's probably been talking to a dozen guys on the phone already tonight. Maybe she's got this habit of calling up guys or something.

"Hi."

"This is Terry. I figured I should call you —"

"Hi!" Again, but this time it's like she's really glad it's me. I wonder if she does that to every guy who calls.

"I figured I should call you and explain about the other night. I must have sounded really dumb."

"Whataya mean?"

"You know, about going for a burger. I must have sounded like a real idiot."

"No, you didn't."

"I probably did. You're just saying that."

Then she didn't say anything, so I'm thinking I better let that drop before I screw it up again. "I would like to go out for a burger sometime. Like, how about Friday night? Eight o'clock? How about A&W? I like it better than McDonald's, don't you?" Right by the paper in front of me, the exact words.

"I have to baby-sit on Friday."

This is where I start to have problems.

"Oh, well."

"How about Saturday?" she says.

"Sure, why not." Then I remember. Saturday night is when I'm supposed to go over to Sean's. We're renting a videotape of that MUSE concert in Madison Square Garden with you in it. We've been weeks trying to get our hands on the tape. And we only got it for that one night.

"I can't. I just remembered I got something planned."

"Maybe some other time, then."

The way she says it, I get the feeling right away that the chance to see her is starting to slip out of my hands. I figure I better do something fast.

"Maybe I could Saturday night, after all. How about seven-thirty?" I figure that should be no problem. I can go over to Sean's later.

"I can't till nine."

Now things are really screwy. For sure Sean's parents are not going out till eight-thirty. And it'd be useless trying to watch it with them around. Then I'm thinking that I don't really know how long we'll be at A&W, and Mom'll probably want me back in the house by eleven-fifteen because she's starting night shift this weekend. All this is going through my head. And she's on the other end of the line waiting for an answer. And the longer I take, the longer she'll have thinking that I don't really want to see her.

"How about Sunday?"

"I can't." Then she says, "How about we leave it till some other time? Call me again next week or something."

"Sure."

I really screwed it up. I can tell.

She starts talking then about something else. Asks me if I have a dog. Man, as if that's all I got on my mind right now — dogs. I say no, I'm not all that crazy about dogs. Which is true but which goes over like a lead balloon, because I can tell after she's been talking for another few minutes that she's crazy about dogs. She has a collie named Brandy, and I go, "Oh yeah," like I'm really interested all of a sudden. And then she tells me about some of the things he can do, like find her when a certain show comes on TV. I say "Oh yeah" a few more times until this rather wonderful conversation ends with me saying, "I didn't know dogs could be that smart. Maybe I should think about getting one."

Then she says good-bye, she's got to go now because her father is complaining that she's always on the phone. And I say sure, I know what you mean. And we hang up. Seven and a half minutes.

Real great stuff, right? A dead slug could have done better. Man, I think I really did the job on myself this time. Girls, I can't handle.

Who cares? There are more important things in life, right?

Right?
Terry

Dear Bruce Springsteen,

I had to write you right away.

Man, the MUSE concert — it knocked me out. It's two hours later and I'm in bed, and I still haven't got over it. I knew you were something else in concert. I mean, I read all about them and I saw the videos, but this was something else. It really blew me away.

We played that part of the tape over about a half-dozen times. I'm not kidding.

"The River," the way you sang it was like it was really something special to you. Like it was you and all those people and you were telling them a story about the way things really are.

It made me think of my mother and the old man. Maybe they felt like that. Who knows?

I was wishing for a while that I was there in the house alone, because after three or four times Sean wasn't getting off on that song much anymore. He wanted to move the tape ahead to the faster ones. I tried to ignore him.

Then "Thunder Road" — that was great, too. I don't understand all what you're trying to say in that song, but I love the way it builds up and builds up and then drives everything home. I love the sax part at the end. The big guy really gives it all he's got.

And then "A Quarter to Three." Wicked, man. Too much. You really get into it. It must be fantastic to let rip like that before all those people. The adrenaline was pumping mad just watching it.

Now I got to see the real thing. I got to get to one of your concerts. I don't know when, and I don't know how I'll get there, but someday I will. No two ways about it.

Hey, and you know what I really got off on, too? The short bit backstage when you were being introduced to some little kid and the way you said hello to him. Like, whataya sayin', man? How ya doin' there? Like you'd say that to anyone, no matter who you met, no matter if they were famous or not.

Man, real fine,
Terry

Dear Bruce Springsteen,

I get in these moods sometimes (a lot lately) where I don't really want to talk to anybody.

Mom hates it. She says nothing'll please me and that I'm a real pain to live with. She tries to talk me out of it and that's the last thing in the world I want. I hate being bugged like that.

Amanda is the one. When she sees that something is getting on my nerves she'll ask those stupid questions. Then the two of us start arguing and before you know it there's a big fuss, and I end up getting mad at her. Sometimes she starts to cry and Mom gets dirty with me, saying I'm four years older than she is and I should have better sense. I take off to the bedroom and slam the door. It's their fault. If they'd just be quiet and leave me alone, it'd be all right.

Today I'm in one of those moods. I never did call Kristy back. I suppose that's part of it. I started going into places where I figured she might be. I saw her yesterday at McDonald's after school. She was with a bunch of girls and she hardly took time to look at me. She went back to talking to them like I never existed. It looked to me like she didn't want the other girls to know that she even noticed I was there.

That's fine with me. If that's the way she wants it, I can forget about her just as quick as she forgot about me. I don't need the hassle.

When I get like this I got no mind for school, least of all math. But I know I got to get cracking at it. It's almost the end of the year, and I sure as hell don't want to flunk it and take a chance on having Jerkins again next year. One year in his class is about all I can stomach, even though he hasn't said much to me since that time about the headband. I guess I cured him. I hauled off 59 on the last test, which brings my average up a bit more. The finals start next week so I got to get myself in gear. Man, I wish math was never invented.

The only thing that keeps me going is the guitar. This is the last week for Kirkland's classes, which is a downer, because he's really been a lot of help to me. He says I'm getting pretty good and I should stick with it. No need to worry about that. I found this book that looks like it's about thirty years old. It's got real exciting stuff in it like "The Red River Valley" and "Skip to My Lou." Must have been the old man's when he was younger.

I still got my mind set on getting an electric. Maybe I'll get lucky and win the lottery. Except I don't want to take a chance on buying tickets with the money I got saved. I spent two bucks last week on those scratch-and-win tickets and never won a thing. A guy in the next apartment building won five thousand bucks last year. Now, wouldn't that be something. Man, I could buy quite the guitar with that kind of dough.

I usually get something for passing. If I do pass, that is. Maybe some long-lost cousin will remember me or something. Who knows? At least I should be able to count on the five bucks I always get in the mail from my grandmother. That'll really boost my savings. For sure Mom'll give me clothes or something, now that she knows what I'd do with money if I had it.

On that exciting note I'll close out and go back to "Red River Valley."

Wake up, the letter is over,
Terry

Dear Bruce Springsteen,

I've been holding off writing till after final exams are over. I had the last one today. Math was yesterday. I think I might do all right. There was only one part of the exam that I know for sure I screwed up.

We got two days off school, and then the killer — year-end report. In the meantime I can sit around and chew my nails. I'm really good at that.

Dad called last night. Mom would never have said nothing, but I could tell by the way she was talking who it was on the other end of the line. When she hung up I could see she wasn't in a very good mood. I sort of stayed around in the living room waiting for her to say something. When she didn't I got a can of pop from the fridge and went to my room. Then, when I knew for sure that Amanda was in bed, I came out again and asked her straight out what he was calling about.

She said, "Not much. He asked about you."

"What did he say?"

"Just asked how you were."

"Did he say if he was coming back, or what?"

"I didn't ask him." She was being pretty snappy.

"Think he will?"

"I doubt it."

"You don't really care, do you?"

"To be quite honest, Terry — no."

That was what I was expecting. But still, it was a lousy way to say it. She could see that I wasn't too pleased. I might have said something I would have been sorry for after, except that she saw it coming and cut me off.

"Okay," she yelled at me, like she had something to prove, "so he's gone. It's not the end of the world. We're managing well enough without him. In fact, a lot better than when he was around. And at least the rent is getting paid on time. No thanks to him, I might add. He keeps saying he'll send some money, but not one red cent has come in the mail from him since the day he took off. He says he's got no money. He's got money for some things though, don't you worry."

I never said nothing at first. Because at first I was wondering if she was right. But then, I couldn't see the old man not thinking enough about us to send money if he had some. I just couldn't believe that.

"Maybe he hasn't got no money, like he said. You don't know. You got to give him a chance."

That got her really mad. "I was giving him a chance for fifteen years! Where did it get us? Stuck in a hole-in-the-wall apartment with about as much future as that stupid band he was playing in!"

I never said nothing else. I knew I'd never get anywhere if I did. I was better off keeping my mouth shut, because we'd only get in a worse fight. Not that there wasn't plenty I could have said. Like, How about me? I feel something for him if she don't. He treated me all right. How about if she tried talking to him, tried to understand why he is like he is instead of getting on his back all the time? Okay, so he's not perfect. Everybody got their faults. Including her. Including me.

Ah, what's the use.
The world is screwed up anyway.

I mean it, it is.
Terry

P.S. I started off writing with my mind made up that it wasn't going to be a downer of a letter like I sent before. Looks like I screwed that up, too.

Dear Bruce Springsteen,

I'm calmed down a bit from the last letter.

Man, I got to ask you something. Did you know when you were my age that one day you'd be really good at what you're doing?

I practice a lot. I know all the chords and everything. I got parts of certain songs down pretty good. I even started fooling around with the idea of writing a song myself. I got one verse and part of another one done.

Then I start thinking my chances of making it one day aren't too good. Man, there must be thousands of guys with dreams and plans just like I got.

I've been listening to some of your old stuff a lot lately. Especially "Growing Up" from *Asbury Park*. I like that song. It took a lot of listening to get at what you're saying, and I still don't think I got it all. But anyway, one thing I do know you're saying in that song is that you got to be your own person and forget about all the crap people fire at you. You got to believe in yourself and stand up for who you are.

I believe that. The people in school who'll have anything to do with me, I can count on one hand. Some of the teachers give me a hard time. Mom and Amanda and me haven't been hitting it off too good lately. But I think I can handle all that. I got my sights set somewhere else, away from this place. One day I'll show them all. Then they'll be wishing they'd treated me better.

I made it through all my exams, in case you're wondering. Math, I got 53. No more Jerkins, and good riddance, too.

Mom said she was happy. She was surprised, I know that for a fact. She tried not to show it. She never said nothing about what she'll give me for passing, and I never asked. But one of these days a new something that I don't need is going to show up in my room. I'm not complaining.

Now I got two months of summer vacation.

So long from the stratosphere,
Terry

Dear Bruce Springsteen,

Man, it's really been hot the last few days. So hot at night that it's hard to sleep. Too hot during the day to stick it in the apartment. We haven't got air conditioning. Summer can be hell sometimes.

I've been spending a lot of time over at Sean's place. It's cooler there. There's a lot of trees in his backyard, and we take the guitars out there and fool around. Sometimes we hang out at the mall for a while. We've been in the music store so many times, the owner calls us by our first names. We've never bought nothing more than a pick or a set of strings, but he don't seem to mind us hanging around. Every time we go in we look at the same guitar, a Fender something like what you got, and wish we had that kind of money. Someday, maybe.

Today the heat really got to us, and we had to go someplace to cool off. We went down to the lake. I wasn't really crazy about going, but Sean kept bugging me. That place is crowded in the summertime. It's the only place anyone can swim. The river, up near the dam, used to be good, but they stopped people from going there after they tested the water and found out all the crap that's in it.

When we showed up at the lake there was hardly room enough to move, there were so many little kids running around, splashing each other and screaming.

We had to get out of there. Sean said he knew the way to another part of the lake, so I followed him a quarter of a mile through the bushes to a place I knew about but I'd never been to before. There were no little kids there but plenty of fellows and girls, some of them our age, a lot of them older. A few of the guys drinking beer looked like they'd been out of school for a couple of years. I recognized some of them. I'd seen them hanging out at the mall or at Napoli's Pizza.

They didn't pay much attention to us, and at first we just hung back to see what was happening. Someone had a box that was blasting out some AC/DC. I used to own the same tape. There were a lot of people out in the water. The ones on shore were mostly girls, lying back on the rocks, drying off in the sun, every now and then smacking at a fly.

Man, some flies get all the breaks. We could have stayed right where we were, staring at those girls. Like the old man used to say about the *Twenty-Minute Workout* girls that came on TV — if they didn't activate your hormones, nothing would. I loved the way the beads of water rolled around on their skin, all nice and tanned, like you're dying to rub your hand across it.

I was really getting off on it, but Sean was practically drooling. Every now and then, when one of the girls would turn over, he'd let out a low groan and start breathing funny. He had me so I couldn't stop laughing. The guy's nuts.

Then this dopehead from school came up to us and started talking.

"Sean, man, how's it goin'? Water's perfect."

"I need something to cool me off," Sean said, rolling his eyes toward the girls.

The guy grinned. "Where you been all the time? Haven't

seen you around much. Remember last summer? Down here every day. Remember Roxanne?" He laughed.

"I dunno. Been busy. You know."

The fellow looked at me like I was the reason. I never said nothing.

"You know, doin' other things," Sean said.

The fellow walked off after a while.

"A real sponge," Sean said when he'd gone.

We went looking for a place to leave our clothes. We stripped off to our trunks. I put my watch and glasses in my sneakers and put them in the bushes.

There were a lot of sharp rocks and twigs and crap around, so the walk to the water was pretty crude. The tan I had ended halfway up my arms, which made me look kind of sick compared to the rest of them. And I'm not exactly muscle-bound to start off with. I must have looked like hell.

It was okay once I got in the water. Because one thing I can do is swim. I took lessons at the pool over at the rec center. It never cost much, and Mom was really set on me knowing how to swim. I might not be much good at most sports, but I do a pretty decent freestyle, and my backstroke isn't bad. I think Sean was surprised, and I hope the others got a good look. I couldn't really tell without my glasses.

We stuck around there most of the afternoon. We came in after a while and lay in the sun. I got the sneakers, and Sean went off and scrounged a beer off one of the guys he knew. We drank that.

Then I caught sight of Kristy. I had no idea she was there. She didn't bother coming over our way, and I sure as hell wasn't going over there and making a fool of myself in front of all those girls. I saw her laughing a few times when I looked over, and I figured she might have been laughing at me. I don't know. I went back in the water after that and kept swimming and swimming till I was halfway across the pond.

Maybe she was wondering whether or not I was in any trouble, I was gone so long.

When I got out of the water I acted like I didn't even notice she was around.

It was getting late then, so we took off home. I guess I still think about her sometimes. She really filled out that swim-suit she was wearing.

Now I got something else on my mind. I got burned to a crisp today. I can hardly move, I'm that sore. I took a cold bath, which helped a bit, and then Mom smothered me with Noxzema. Man, it hurts. I know I'm not going to be able to sleep.

I'm on fire (but hell, it ain't funny),
Terry

Dear Bruce Springsteen,

I just been sitting in the living room, peeling off dead skin. It really grossed Amanda out.

Guess what? I got a letter today from the old man. Not only that, but a twenty-dollar bill. It wasn't much of a letter. A note is more like it. He said he's fine and he hopes he'll see me before long. That was about it. It's hard to imagine the old man ever writing a long letter.

He sent the same thing to Amanda. Mom got a money order for a hundred bucks. Enough for one trip to the supermarket, she said. At least it's something. She'd probably complain no matter how much it was. It shows he's thinking about us. Mom never said nothing when I told her that.

I got to go. I called Sean and he's coming over in a few minutes. We're going to see this guy who's got a guitar and amp for sale.

Fingers crossed,
Terry

Dear Bruce Springsteen,

Riding high, man, ridin' high.

Man, you're not going to believe this. I got a guitar and amp, both of them for eighty-five bucks. I can hardly believe it myself and I'm staring right at the two suckers right here in my bedroom, now.

I'll admit they're not great. Probably a pawnshop job from years ago. But, like Sean said, it's a wicked deal for eighty-five bucks.

I'd seen this notice on the bulletin board over in the mall where people stick up notes if they got things for sale. It said 125 bucks. I figured, no way have I got that kind of dough, but I pulled off one of the tags with the telephone number on it, anyway. Then yesterday when I got the money from the old man, I figured what the hell, that makes sixty bucks with what I got saved, I'll go see him. I thought maybe he'd sell me just the guitar. No way, both of them or nothing. I tried them out and they sounded pretty good. Then he cut the price by ten bucks.

This got me thinking — the guy's desperate. He's moving out of his apartment. The furniture is gone. All the rest of his stuff is packed up and ready to go. He looks like he needs money. Maybe I can get his price down some more.

Then I started saying to Sean that I really don't think it's worth it — $115 for that.

Sean caught my eye. Then he started finding scratches and stuff on them and saying the guitar really needed new strings. "Man," he said, "I don't know if it's worth it."

That got him down to a hundred. He wouldn't budge from there.

I said, "Sixty bucks and anything else I got, you can have."

"Like what?"

"I dunno. A watch." That's what they all say, right? After I said it, I started thinking, the old lady would have my neck if she knew I'd traded away the watch she gave me for Christmas last year.

"A watch is the last thing I need."

"How about some tapes?" Sean said to him, but looking at me. "You got a whole bunch he'd like." Then we started naming off all the tapes I had back in the apartment that I didn't play anymore.

"Bring them over, and I'll have a look. I got a long drive ahead of me. But I gotta have more cash."

So we took off and went back to the apartment. On our way Sean offered me a loan of twenty-five bucks, without me even asking him. I didn't want to take it at first because he said yesterday he's been saving money for a bass. But he said that this was too good a chance to pass up. I took it, but I promised to get it back to him as soon as I could. If he hadn't loaned me the money I don't know what I would have done. I thought of asking Amanda, but I know I would have got nowhere fast with that.

So, to make a long story short, I got the guitar and the amp for eighty-five bucks plus seven or eight tapes. I call that a good deal. They're not great, but it's a start. Compared to what we been looking at in the music store, they're crap, right. But at least you plug it in and it makes a good noise. It should really stir up some fun between me and Mrs. Mac-Kinnon next door.

What's great, too, is the way Sean helped me out when I needed him. He's turned out to be a real great guy to buddy around with. When he gets that bass now, we'll really be in business.

I better go. I've got a couple of hours before Mom gets off work. She don't know yet that I got it.

I hear you're still in England. Take it easy.

Signing off and plugging in,
Terry

Dear Bruce Springsteen,

I really been working hard to get down "I'm On Fire." I got most of it. I been thinking about giving Kirkland a call to see if he'd give me a hand.

Mom found out about the guitar and amp that night after she came home from work. She came into the bedroom to tell me something and saw them there. She wasn't exactly pleased, but she never let loose at me like I figured she would. I think she half expected it. She wanted to know where I got the money. When I told her, she went on and on about borrowing money when I didn't know how I was going to pay it back.

Then I said staying home with Amanda should be worth something, which didn't go over so hot, because I'd never said anything about that before. It was just taken for granted I had to do it, my part to help out so she could go out to her job. It was stupid—I never should have said anything. I tried to back out of it, but she wouldn't let me, till finally I got dirty and started yelling and telling her to just leave me alone.

I know, I know, I never should have said what I did, but she didn't have to keep bugging me about it. Anyway, Amanda is getting to be a real pain to baby-sit. She never listens to what I say anymore. And when Sean is in the house and I'm supposed to be looking after her, she acts like such an idiot, it's embarrassing. And she never wants to watch what we want to watch on TV.

That little blowup was a few nights ago. Since then things have almost got back to normal. Normal, right now, is still not very good.

Mom said today, "I hope to God it's just a stage you're goin' through." Like it's all my fault. I almost said that I wished the old man was around. But I never said nothing. I've learned to keep my mouth shut.

Enough about my family. You must be getting pretty sick of me blabbering on and on like you know them or something. The only reason I kept writing these letters was because it helped me work things out in my head. Now it's got to be a habit. It don't bother me that I'm not getting any answers to them. I told you when I started that I didn't really expect to. Maybe if I did I'd have to quit writing because I'd feel I was taking up too much of your time. Right now I can look at the poster of you on the wall and think, hey, someday that guy, when he gets some time, might look at his mail and discover this guy, me, and find out all about him.

That's all. It's no big deal if it don't happen. I'm not really counting on it. If you don't, fine. I can handle it. I know you got more important things to be doing.

No sweat,
Terry

Dear Bruce Springsteen,

I spent almost the whole afternoon in front of Sean's TV set watching a tape of Live Aid. Today is the anniversary of the concert.

I got to tell you right off, though, that I'm still kind of disappointed you weren't there. You would have blown them away. I know you give a lot of money to charity, so I thought it was really something you would have wanted to do. I guess you were busy with other things.

The band I liked the best was The Who. I wish they were still together. And U2 — they were excellent.

The whole thing got me thinking again about how bad off some people are. It was great to see rock musicians helping out the way they did. Me and Sean were saying that it really must have been something to be a part of a concert like that.

Then tonight we called up Kirkland and went over to his place with the guitars to get his help on a few songs. And we got to talking about how great it would be if we were good enough that we could put on a concert, like to raise money for a charity or something. We got to talking some more, and after a while I came up with this idea.

I don't know if it would work, but it really got me going. Why not just do a lip-sync concert? Set up a stereo system and have people do take-offs on different groups and singers, like it was a real concert. It's really big in some places. I've seen it on TV. Maybe have a few people singing for real, too. I think it would go over. We wouldn't charge much, maybe just a couple of bucks. I think people would pay that much when they knew it was for a good cause. Kirkland said he thought there'd be lots of people at school who'd want to take part. He said he'd sing for real himself.

We talked about who we could give the money to. There's lots of charities who could use it. Kirkland mentioned three or four. Then I thought about the Smiths and how desperate they are. I told Sean and Kirkland if the concert did go ahead, then that would be a really good place for the money to go. They didn't need much convincing.

We're going to think about the whole thing over the summer and get back to him when school opens again. He said he'd be willing to give us a hand organizing it.

Man, I can really picture it now. I already know who I'd do. Give you one guess.

You're right,
Terry

Dear Bruce Springsteen,

It's been almost two weeks now since the last time I wrote. This is almost the longest ever between letters. There's a good reason for it — plenty of them, actually.

I put it off and put it off — writing I mean — because I almost had myself convinced that what I was doing was really stupid. Writing to you as if you'd care about what happens to me. You must get all kinds of letters, some from real sickos, and I probably sound like one of them. Man, I'm not a kid anymore, I should be able to handle things myself.

I'm not sure if anybody really gives a damn about me and how I feel. If they do, they sure got a funny way of showing it.

It started last Saturday when this guy named Nick showed up for supper. I had no idea he was coming. When I came home about five o'clock in the afternoon, there he was sitting down on the sofa playing some card game with Amanda and laughing over some stupid remark she'd made. I thought at first it must have been a relative I'd never seen before. But it turned out that it was this guy Mom met somewhere or other and had invited over for a meal. I wouldn't exactly call him a boyfriend, but they're not just friends, either. The thing that gets me is that she never even let me know he was coming. She could've at least warned me.

At supper I didn't say much. I was polite enough, but he got the message that I wasn't exactly overjoyed that he was around. He tried to talk to me about baseball, and when that didn't work, he came out with this wonderful line about what did I think of Madonna, like I was dying to talk about music. I said, not much, and of course Amanda suddenly gets all excited and says she loves Madonna and thinks the way she dresses is great and after supper would he like to see all the pictures she's got of her. The way he answered her, I knew he had to be faking it. I think he's a real jerk.

After dessert I went to my room and I stayed there for half an hour. Then I went outdoors again. I never said a word to anybody when I left the house.

Three hours later, when I got back, he was gone. The old lady should have known from the look I gave her that I didn't want to talk about it.

I started walking toward my room, and she said, "You're behaving like a child."

I slammed the door behind me.

Before long she had the door open. "He's only a friend," she said.

"Some friend."

"You don't even know him."

"I don't want to know him."

"What's that supposed to mean?"

I never said nothing.

"My God, Terry, grow up. Quit acting like a kid if you expect to be treated like an adult. You didn't have the courtesy to carry on a sensible conversation."

I just sat there. Man, she knows how I feel.

"Well?" she said. "Don't go jumping to conclusions over something you don't know anything about."

"How am I supposed to know anything?"

"Ask, and you might find out!"

When I didn't answer, she said, "Why don't we talk about it?"

I didn't move a muscle. And finally she went out, but left the door halfway open.

I got up and shut it the rest of the way myself.

Man, I hate this. I really do.

We were never like this before. When Dad was around, I never remember once when we argued like we do now. I think she depended on me to help her get through the rough times with the old man. We got along. We really did.

I can't win in this situation. I won't be satisfied till the old man at least starts showing up once in a while. And if he does come back, it'll probably only mean more of a fuss than we got now. Either way, it's hell for me. I wish I was older and out on my own.

There's no one I can talk to about this. That's why you're getting these crappy letters.

Okay?
Terry

Dear Bruce Springsteen,

I been trying to keep practicing. Some days I don't feel like doing much. It's a big decision just to get out of bed. When I start fooling around with the guitar, it's better. I remember you saying that music saved your life. I don't know if it'll save mine, but it's about the only thing I got right now. If it wasn't for that I'd be royally screwed up.

Yesterday Mom gave me thirty bucks and told me to pay off whatever I still owed Sean and keep the rest. I wasn't going to take it at first, but I could see she was doing it to try to patch things up between us, so I figured I might as well. It was the least I could do.

I went over to Sean's to pay him back, but he wasn't home. His mother and father were sitting together on the deck out in back laughing about something. They said they thought he'd gone swimming. That really bugged me because I figured he'd phone before going down there, to see if I wanted to go. That's what he always did before. I gave his mother the money to give to him.

I found out later he'd gone there with Tonya, this girl he's interested in. I wouldn't say that's going to work out. She changes boyfriends like some people change clothes. And she's not Sean's type. I tried to tell him that, but he can't see it. He thinks if she just gets to know him, everything will be fine.

That leaves me with nothing to do, more time to think about what a great time I'm having with my life.

I hung around Shankland Field this afternoon for a while and watched part of a baseball tournament. I need to get involved in something like that. It would get my mind off things. If I was a better player or I didn't mind screwing up a few games, then I might.

Eventually I bought a can of pop and some fries and sat in the back row of the bleachers, as far away from everyone as I could get.

Sean called tonight to tell me where he'd been. He went on and on like it was the greatest thing that ever happened to him. Big deal. Then he said I should call up Kristy and ask her out. He said Tonya and her were good friends and Tonya thought that she really liked me. I don't believe that for a minute. He said we should go out somewhere together, the four of us.

I said I'd think about it, which I'm doing right now. I don't know. I loused it up before and I'd probably do it again. I really don't think she likes me, anyway. I think it's all a bluff. If she did, then she'd be doing more to let me know.

That works two ways, don't it. Maybe I should make the first move this time. I don't know. Man, I wish to hell there were a few more straightforward things in this world.

Up in the air. Again.
Terry

Dear Bruce Springsteen,

I called up Kristy. (I had to do something. I was going crazy thinking about myself.) I couldn't go through all that crap of getting up the nerve to call like I did last time. I said to myself, you got to make up your mind one way or the other and stick to it. She either says yes or she says no. No more of this stupid fooling around.

So I went to the phone and dragged it into the bathroom again and dialed right away. I knew what I was going to say, and I figured I knew what her answer was going to be.

She said hello.

"Hi, this is Terry. I'm calling to see if you want to go out with me tomorrow night to the movie. Sean and Tonya are going. All four of us could go together." Everything said, straightforward, to the point, no screw-up.

"Sure, I'd love to. What time?"

And I just about dropped the phone. I wasn't expecting it. Not like that, anyway, so quick.

"Eight o'clock. No, seven, if we're going to the early show. I'd better check with Sean. I'll call you back."

"Sure."

"Okay. Well, okay, I'll talk to you later. See ya."

"Okay."

That was it. We hung up.

I thought afterward, Blanchard, there's really something wrong with you. Here you had the girl on the phone. She was agreeing with everything you said. The least you could have done was talk to her for a few minutes. You could have said something instead of just hanging up like some idiot. Man, you could have talked about dogs or something.

But I couldn't think of anything to say, honest. Of course a million lousy things came to me the second the receiver hit the button, but right when I needed to, I couldn't think of a thing.

I called up Sean and we set the time. Then I was an hour getting up the nerve to phone her back. And when I did finally dial, she wasn't home. To tell the truth, it was a relief. I left the message with her mother about the time.

Now I got to spend the whole evening with her, playing the real cool guy that I am. No sweat, right? If you can do it, I can do it.

Wish me luck (for sure I'll need it),
Terry

Dear Bruce Springsteen,

I think I loused it up—the date with Kristy. I know I loused it up. Real sweet. I don't think she'd ever go out with me again. I might as well face it — when it comes to girls, I'm sad, real sad.

It wasn't all a screw-up. The movie part was all right. Even going for something to eat afterward went okay. I wasn't a dead loss for something to say like I figured I'd be. Having two other people there helped. We talked about the movie and music most of the time. I mean I probably sounded like I had a brain.

But when it came to walking her home afterward, that's where I blew it. With just the two of us, my half of the conversation dried up till it must have sounded like my tongue had a shot of novacaine or something. When we got to her house and were standing outside the back door, this was where I really must have looked cool — hardly getting a word out, nervous as hell about what I should do and when I should do it, half grinning like I had everything under control when we both knew I never did.

I was there so long not doing anything, she finally said she had to go in and *she* leaned over and kissed *me*. Hard on the mouth. It must have been like kissing a corpse, I was that stiff. Hell, I almost lost my balance.

Man, I can't believe I was that much of a jerk. I'm sure I was worse than any of those nerds you see in the movies. She must have had a good laugh for herself when she went inside. I would've if I'd been her.

But I sure as hell wasn't laughing. I was cursing myself all the way home. You wouldn't think anybody could be so dumb. I knew what to do. I practiced it all in my head, every bit of it. And I knew what I felt like doing. But put me in the real situation, and I screw it up worse than if I had pasta for a brain.

Enough about that. I just want to forget about it. I thought that by getting it down on paper I'd see that maybe it wasn't so bad as I thought it was.

It was worse.

Like I said before, I don't really need a girl, anyway. Besides, I can't afford it. I'm back to being broke again. And what do I have to show for it—a look on my face worse than if I'd been sucking lemons for six months.

Forget it,
Terry

P.S. Man, I must sound to you like a real winner. Go ahead, have a laugh. I wouldn't blame you.

Dear Bruce Springsteen,

She said she'd call. She never did. I saw her in the mall yesterday. When she saw me coming, she made out like she never noticed and turned right into another aisle. Probably every girl she hangs out with knows about it now. I don't want to talk about it anymore.

I've taken up lifting weights. I looked at myself in the mirror the other night and I thought, man, I got to do something about this mess of skin and bones I call a body. It don't know the meaning of the word *muscle*. I should be ashamed to take off my shirt in public. No wonder girls avoid me like I got VD.

Sean's got a set of barbells and a bench. He hasn't used them for a while, but I convinced him that we should set them up in his basement again and start working out.

I looked at some of the pictures of you before you got into your workout program, and don't mind me saying this, but you did look pretty scrawny. Now look at you. You should hear what I've heard girls say about your body. Even my mother can't take her eyes off you when she sees you dancing around onstage in those videos. She likes the way you have your sleeves rolled up. Thinks it's sexy. I never figured she noticed things like that.

Sean's been spending a lot of time lately with Tonya, but we do manage to work out pretty often. He came across this list of exercises all diagrammed out that we use. We put it on the wall in the basement, and we go through that, sometimes two or three times in a row. I found it tough going at first, till I cut down on the weight on the bar to give myself chance to build up my strength. Now it's not so bad. And I can notice a difference, too. Maybe I'm dreaming, but I can feel muscle hardening up. No kidding. By the end of the summer, who knows? I might be wearing cutoff T-shirts. We got no plans to get like the body-builders you see on TV, all greased up. I think that's pretty gross.

Sean *is* spending a lot of time with Tonya. That's his business, I guess. He says I should try and see Kristy again. Says you can't expect much from one date. I said, "Are you kidding? She's got a lot more things on her mind than me. Forget it, man, I'm not going through all that again. Case closed." I'd never tell him the whole story.

It seems to me that I'm more into guitar now than he is, although we still work in some time to practice together. He's got other things on his mind. I'm not sure anymore if he'll stick it out to the time when we can get a band together. He says he will, but I figure that might be a bit of a bluff. Even this lip-sync concert—he don't talk about it like he's excited, not like first when the idea came up.

I sure am—in fact, I've even gone to see the Smiths about it. Took a bit of nerve, but I had to do it. We couldn't really go ahead and say where the money was going without their okay.

When I knocked two little kids came running to the door. They stood there staring at me without saying a word till their father showed up. He recognized me from being around the neighbourhood, but I could tell he didn't really know who I was. I told him my name and where I lived and asked him if I could talk to him and his wife for a minute. He said sure, to come on in, and he made a joke about there not being many places to sit down.

He seemed like a nice kind of guy, pretty easygoing, especially when you think about what happened to them. His wife was there in the kitchen. She looked kind of down, and she never tried to hide it. She was sitting at the table smoking a cigarette.

I hardly knew how to ask them because I knew some people might take it as an insult to be offered money like that. I tried to make it sound like it was something we were going to do anyway for fun, and we weren't sure what we could do with the money if we made any, and perhaps they could use it.

Neither one of them said anything at first. The fellow looked at his wife, trying, I guess, to figure out what was going through her mind.

Then she said, "Sure. Lord knows we could use it. The kids still haven't got proper beds. As long as there's no big deal made about it. I wouldn't want everybody to think we're looking for handouts."

I promised her I'd make sure of that. Her husband was real pleased, I could see it when I got up to leave. He wanted me to stay longer and have a cup of coffee or something, but I said that I'd better go. I promised I'd come back before long just for a visit.

It's great to feel good about something for a change.

Real good,
Terry

Dear Bruce Springsteen,

Maybe you been wondering what's been happening with Mom and that fellow. I been wondering, too, but I haven't said nothing to her about it. He hasn't been in the house since, and she's never said a word about him. Let's hope it stays that way.

Not that I haven't been thinking a lot about it. In fact, I'm all the time thinking what I would do if Mom got really serious about him. It didn't seem to bother Amanda like it bothered me that time he came to supper. Maybe I made too much of it.

I been trying to see Mom's side of this, but it don't make no sense to me. It's like she's already given up on the old man. And all she wants is for him to send her money and leave her alone. Man, you just can't forget about that part of your life like it never happened. Okay, so he mightn't have been very good to her sometimes, but that's no reason not to try to work things out. Maybe he's willing to change. She don't think he is, but she don't know that. She's not even willing to give him a chance.

What I really wish is that Dad was around so we could straighten things out. If he only knew what was going on, I bet he'd be here tomorrow.

I got to admit that I thought he would have called again, or wrote. Maybe he did and Mom never said nothing about it. I wouldn't be surprised. It's hard to think that he don't really care enough to do that. I'd say there's something fishy about all this, something I don't know nothing about.

Maybe it means they're splitting up for good. It's got to the point where now I'm starting to worry about that. If it did happen, I wouldn't have to live with Mom — there's no law that says I would. Maybe I'd leave and track down the old man and stay with him. Who knows?

I'm not saying that I don't like Mom. It's just that we haven't been seeing eye to eye lately. And I can see it getting worse. There's a lot about the old man and me that Mom don't really understand. She don't see that, or she's not willing to admit it.

Dad and me, we've never really had a fair chance to spend enough time together. Alone, I mean, to talk about all this.

That's all I guess I got to say,
Terry

Dear Bruce Springsteen,

Summer can really drag sometimes. I need more to do, a job or something. It's starting to get boring. Man, it gets on my nerves spending so much time just hanging around the apartment and walking the streets. Sean is gone camping with his family for a few days.

I think I told you before I was working on a song. What do you think of these lyrics?

> Summer's heat, driving me crazy
> driving me down, not getting me through
> Fire's burning in and out of me
> I can't escape, I need to talk to you
> C'mon, girl, I gotta talk to you
>
> I need a route, a long cool tunnel
> a one-way ticket to the promised land
> I need a reason to make things happen
> I need a reason just to make some plans
> C'mon, girl, I need to talk to you
> Yeah, c'mon, Rhonda, I gotta talk to you

I need you more than you need a reason
for me running hot, calling your name
I need you now, tomorrow is later
and later never pays in the freedom game
C'mon, girl, I gotta talk to you
Yeah, c'mon, Rhonda, I gotta talk to you

That's all I got done so far. I don't really know a girl named Rhonda. I guess it could mean any girl.

I got an idea for the third verse — how running makes the fire worse — but I haven't worked it out yet.

I've taped myself playing guitar and singing it. When I played it back I wasn't so sure. The way I sing, it sounds like someone else's style. I should have my own style. I'm never going to get anywhere sounding like someone else. I guess that takes a while.

The lyrics probably sound really crappy to you, someone who knows what they're doing when they write a song. Anyway, it's a start. We all got to start somewhere.

Hot off the pen of
Terry

Dear Bruce Springsteen,

Sean got back last night. He told me all about the great time he had with this girl he met in one of the campgrounds. Showed me the hickeys to prove it.

I wish I could go someplace for a vacation. We used to go camping when I was younger. We'd pack up the old van and take off somewhere. We'd never plan much where we were going, just drive till Dad decided to stop. Once we ended up in Nova Scotia. I guess those days are over. Mom said when she gets her vacation, we'll go somewhere if we can afford it. That's a big "if." Besides, she can't take her vacation till November, when school is open, and we won't be able to go then, anyway.

I remember once when we were camping in this park somewhere, Mom thought there was a bear on the loose. It was three o'clock in the morning and all of a sudden we heard this godawful noise outside the tent, something knocking over pots and stuff out by the picnic table. Mom let out a vicious scream that must have woke up half the campground. Dad put his head out through the flap and took a look outside the tent with the flashlight, just in time to see a couple of squirrels tear off through the woods. Only he didn't tell Mom right away what it was. When he did tell her, we had a big laugh about it, although Mom didn't think it was very funny at first, especially when she had to explain it to the mess of people who came over to see what the hell was going on.

We all laughed about it after. I can remember that trip like it was yesterday.

This afternoon, before Tonya showed up, me and Sean were back at the weights. A few days away from them, and you sure notice it. When Sean was gone I was doing sit-ups and push-ups to keep in shape, but it's not the same. The weights can really make you sweat.

We talked a lot about the concert idea. Sean says he's not so sure about it anymore. I knew it. He's afraid we'll look really dumb if we screw it up. And he said he don't think people would be getting much for their money. I told him, man, that's our job, to see that didn't happen. I told him I'd already gone to see the Smiths and they're counting on it. I think maybe I convinced him we got to go ahead with it.

To tell the truth, it's starting to get to me, too — thinking about how to organize the whole thing so it runs off right. But I still really want to go through with it.

The only thing we can do now is talk it up a bit. Not give any of the details yet, like who the money is going to and stuff, but try and work up some interest so that when school gets going again, people'll be all psyched up about it. We told Tonya. I wouldn't say this to Sean, but that was as good as announcing it on the radio.

I'll keep you posted.

> Your friend, the concert promoter,
> *Terry*

Dear Bruce Springsteen,

They're getting a divorce.

I would have figured I'd be mad. I'm not. I'm sick. I'm sitting here in my room like a lump, trying to think what I should do. Man, I can't handle this.

When she came into my room I could tell by the look on her face that something was up. She closed the door behind her, which she never does. I turned down the ghetto blaster.

"I need to talk to you alone," she said.

I never said nothing. I looked at her. I didn't know what to expect.

I was sitting up at the head of the bed. She sat down at the foot. I had just made up the bed from the night before.

"We don't seem to talk much anymore," she said. "I used to like those talks. I thought we knew each other then, and now I'm not so sure."

I kind of shrugged.

"I guess you've changed," she said.

"You have, too."

"I still love you just as much."

Then I knew for sure something was up. I was almost embarrassed. She said it like it was true, but she also said it like she had it thought out before she came in the room. I couldn't bring myself to look at her straight in the face.

"This is going to hurt you, no matter how I tell you."

I stared at her.

"Your father and I are getting a divorce."

When I finally said something all that came out was, "I'm not surprised." It came out almost automatically, like I'd practiced it.

"Now don't get mad. It's the best thing for both of us and for you and Amanda, too."

I must have looked really stunned.

"I know it is. Your father and I would never get back together. It's just as well to make it final."

"It's because of that guy, isn't it?"

"No, Terry, it's not."

I could almost tell for sure that what she was saying wasn't true. "I bet it is," I said.

She never said nothing. She just shook her head for a few seconds.

"You do what you want," I said. That came out, too, like I hardly had to think about what I was saying. I don't know myself how I meant it.

"Whatever happens, there's nothing for you to worry about. Everything'll work out."

She left after that. I guess because I didn't say much else.

Nothing for me to worry about.

What does the old man think of all this? How come I'm not getting any answers from him? Someone tell me that.

Terry

Dear Bruce Springsteen,

I've had more time to think about what's happened. It didn't help.

Man, even when I'm out somewhere, away from the apartment, it's still in the back of my mind. I can't enjoy myself much anymore.

Sean must figure something is up, but he won't ask. He knows I don't want to talk to him about it. I'm not sure why. I guess I don't want anybody to think that there's anything wrong. Everybody else's life seems normal enough — why not mine?

I'm thinking about doing something, and the only person I'm going to tell is you. And since you're so far away and since you'll probably never read this anyway, it don't matter much.

I'm thinking about taking off and seeing if I can't track down the old man. What have I got to lose?

This afternoon, while Mom and Amanda were gone to the grocery store, I poked around in Mom's bedroom till I found the letter he sent her that time with the hundred bucks in it. There was no return address anywhere, but the postmark

on the envelope was clear enough. It was just what I figured
— Callum.

At first I wasn't going to read the letter. I had it put back
in the drawer and covered up like I found it. But then I went
back in and dug it out again. There was nothing much on it.
Just a few lines, no longer than the letter he wrote to me.
Like I said, the old man was never one for writing letters.

Perhaps that runs in the family. Because now I'm stuck for
something else to say. There's only one thing I got on my
mind and I already told you what it is.

That's all,
Terry

Dear Bruce Springsteen,

I haven't gone yet. I almost took off this morning. But I chickened out. I won't tomorrow morning, though.

I never done nothing like this before. I'm a bit scared, to tell the truth.

I've done a lot of planning for it. I got my hands on a road map, and I know exactly where I'm going and how I'm going to get there. Callum is about 150 miles away. I'll see how far I can get hitchhiking, but if I got to, I can take a bus. I haven't got much money, even with what I borrowed from Sean.

I guess what scares me more than anything is thinking about what I might find once I get there. But I'm going through with it. Nothing is going to stop me now. That guy Nick showed up in the house again today. He wasn't there long. He drove Mom home from work, and then he came in for a few minutes. She invited him to stay for supper, but he wouldn't. I didn't say anything to him that made him feel welcome. I hope he got the message.

After he left, Mom gave me a few dirty looks, but she never said nothing. But she never made much of a supper, either, which I guess said a lot.

It's not that I don't like her anymore. I just wish all this had never happened, that things were back like they were before the old man left. They were never great, but they were a lot better than they are now.

Wish me luck,
Terry

Dear Bruce Springsteen,

I hope you don't mind long letters because a lot has happened since this morning.

I'm writing this in the apartment in Callum where Dad (and this woman Charlene) have been living. It's not much of a place. It's small and not in such hot shape. It could use a good cleaning up.

I ended up here tonight, after a long trip and a long time tracking down the old man.

I left the house about ten o'clock this morning. I told Mom I was going over to Sean's and that I wouldn't be home for lunch. All she said was to be sure to be back by three-thirty. She's working evenings and had to be at work by four. I walked around the house and picked up the backpack I had thrown out of my bedroom window. It never had much in it—a change of clothes and my toothbrush and stuff.

Then I walked for about twenty-five minutes, until I got to the highway. It was another hour before anybody picked me up. The guy was only going about ten miles but that was okay. A ride is a ride. He didn't talk much, which suited me fine. It was the second ride that gave me a hell of a fright.

I wasn't going to get in with them at first because they

looked really dragged out, but I figured I might be stuck where I was forevermore if I started getting choosy. I wasn't in the car two minutes, though, before I realized I was taking a chance I should never have been taking. The old lady would've had a fit if she knew.

There was three of them in an old Mustang, all guys, all of them older than me. Two were maybe twenty, and one fellow looked like he was about sixteen. It was hard to tell. He was crumpled up in the backseat next to me, asleep.

After I got in, the guy who was driving said, "Keep your window down. Pete back there puked up his guts. We scraped him off, but he still stinks. That's what he gets for trying to chug hard liquor." The guy in the passenger seat next to him started to laugh.

I could see it then, dried on his shirt. Enough to make me want to puke myself. I tried to think about something else, but the stink kept bringing me back to it.

The two fellows up front didn't look like they were drunk. Just really dragged out, like I said. The fellow in the passenger seat kept nodding off, then waking up for a few minutes, and then nodding off again. What scared me was thinking that the guy driving might fall asleep, too, and put us off the road. He was driving pretty fast. We might've all ended up dead.

I searched around for a seat belt without giving away what I was doing. I could only find one end. The part it buckled into must have been down between the seats somewhere or under that other guy. I was getting more and more nervous all the time.

The guy that was driving asked me a few questions when I first got aboard, like where I was going and stuff like that, but after he saw that I wasn't much of a talker, he didn't bother with it anymore. Now I started piling the questions to him, not that I wanted to be doing it, but because I figured maybe it would help keep him awake.

They were headed for a place that's a couple of hundred miles past Callum. "We're going there to look for work. The boys gave us a little send-off party last night before we left. I got maybe two hours' sleep."

Wonderful. That's all I needed to hear. Now I knew for sure I had to keep him talking.

I surprised myself. I shot the bull with this guy off and on for almost an hour. I found out that I could really fake it — talking like I went to booze parties every weekend and fooled around with girls and couldn't wait for the day I could buy myself a brand-new Corvette.

Probably I wasn't that good, but the guy never had all his senses anyway, and to him I sounded like I was for real. Actually, he turned out to be a half-decent fellow. He was nice enough to me.

The thing I still wasn't getting off on, though, was the way he was driving. Man, twice he passed cars on a solid line. After that I tried to get him to slow down. I told him that the stretch of road we were driving on was a bad place for cops, that a friend of my old man's had been caught there twice in one week, which was crap of course, but I had to do something.

What helped me, too, was your music. I got him talking about you, and once I found out that he really liked certain songs, I had lots to say to keep his mind off driving so fast. I told him all kinds of things about you that he never knew, like how you came to write some of the songs that he liked. I had him convinced he should buy *Nebraska*.

In the end he said, "I like the guy. He's got some real good drivin' music. But I still like Seger better." I'm sure you can handle that.

By then we'd come to a small town about forty miles from Callum. I knew they had to stop for gas. I had my mind made up miles back that I was getting out there. When he hauled up in front of the pumps I said I was going to call a friend of mine who lived there and I was going to his place for a few hours.

The guy said sure, take it easy. When I was getting out of the car I told him again to buy that album. I gave him a fast good-bye and the same to his buddy in the front seat. The guy in the back with the vomit shirt still hadn't moved.

I waited in the phone booth till they had gone off down the highway again, and then I asked the guy pumping gas where the bus to Callum stopped. It wasn't far. It took me about ten minutes to walk there.

I'd made up my mind to take the bus the rest of the way. That ride had freaked me a bit. Why push my luck? It would be a three-hour wait till the right bus came along, but I was in no hurry. I figured I'd rather get where I was going in one piece. I don't hitchhike much. Maybe I need more getting used to it.

The bus ride was just the opposite — really boring. Except that I had all kinds of things on my mind, like was I doing the right thing and was Mom getting worried yet and what do I do if I can't get in touch with the old man? Pretty depressing stuff till I made up my mind that there was no other way and turning back would only make it worse.

When the bus got into the station I went straight to a pay phone and dug through the book till I found BJ's. I wasn't looking for the phone number, just the name of the street it was on.

I went out in front of the station, looked up the street in one direction and then the other, and wondered what I should do. I started to walk toward the part of the city that looked like it had the most traffic. After a while I wised up and asked someone for directions.

It was almost an hour before I finally got in sight of the club. The last part of the walk took me past half a dozen restaurants and fast-food joints. I gave in to breaking another five-dollar bill and bought myself some fries. They kept me from having to go into BJ's right away. I figured I needed a few minutes to gear myself up for that.

Just inside the front door was a sign that said "No Minors Allowed." I never paid it no attention. It was really black inside, I guess because I just came out of the sunlight. The only real light was over the bar and in the corner where the pool tables were. There weren't many people around, a couple of guys shooting pool and a few more standing up around the bar. I gave my eyes a minute or so to get used to it, and then I strolled past all the empty tables to the bar.

The bartender looked at me like I'd better have a good excuse for being there. Before he had a chance to chew me out I asked to see the manager. He said the manager wasn't there. So I told him who I was looking for and asked him if he knew where I could find him. By now everyone in the place was staring at me.

"He's my father."

"Yeah." The bartender raised his eyebrows and stuck out his lower lip. "You're sure?"

I waited, without answering such a stupid question.

"The guy knows his own father, Tom," one of the fellows standing at the bar said.

"Where can I find him?" I asked again.

"He lives in Birchwood Apartments. Which one, I don't know."

I didn't wait around. I got out of there while I was ahead of the game.

Back out in the sunshine, I stopped three people before I found someone who could tell me how to get there.

Lucky it wasn't too far away. It took twenty minutes. None of what I'd been doing all day seemed real until I saw the apartment building. Then it hit me — this is it. All the things I'd practiced in my mind that I wanted to say to him came rushing at me, screwing up my head and making me nervous. I shouldn't have been nervous about my own father.

The apartment building is not much to look at from the outside. It needs a paint job real bad. And it could do with a lawn and a few trees. I could tell from the lobby that the inside wasn't going to be any better.

I waited in the lobby till someone came around. There were names on some of the mailboxes but none with the old man's name. 106 had "Charlene Symonds" on it. A woman came in from a taxi with a load of groceries. I opened the outside door for her. While she was searching her purse for a key, I asked her if she knew what apartment he lived in. She told me the basement, 106 she thought it was. I told her he was my father, and when I walked through the open door behind her, she never said nothing.

There was nothing to do, only go to the apartment and ring the buzzer. When I got there, I pressed it twice. I knew it rang inside because I could hear it. I knocked, and there was still no answer. I looked at my watch. It was almost seven-thirty. I sat on the floor with my back against the wall and waited. Every time I heard anyone walking my way, I stood up.

It was more than an hour before I saw him coming. He was wearing the same baseball cap he always wore. New jeans, but the same Budweiser belt buckle. There was a woman walking a half-step behind him.

I looked away as he got closer. He didn't really notice who I was till he was almost to the door.

"Terry," he said. "My good God!"

He put one arm around my shoulder and pulled me in tight to him.

"Where in the world did you come from?"

All I could do was smile. I didn't know how to say it.

"You've grown. You're taller. Hell, man, it's real good to see ya!"

"Good to see you."

He was waiting for more. I shrugged, relieved, I guess, by all the fuss he made about me.

"Well then, grab your knapsack, come on in," he said as he turned to unlock the door. "This is Charlene," he said. I guess she figured out who I was.

"Excuse the mess," she said.

The place was pretty grungy. Still is. It looks like it hasn't been cleared away for weeks.

The old man, of course, wanted to know all about how I got there. When he found out that Mom didn't know anything about it, he called home and told her where I was. He wanted me to talk to her, but I wouldn't. I knew she'd be calling back before long. Tomorrow probably, knowing Mom. And by then she'd be calmed down, maybe.

He was starved for news. I sat in the living room, and we talked and talked for a long time. Until Charlene came out of the bathroom all dressed up and told him what time it was. He had to get ready. He's in a band, like I figured, and they're playing tonight.

He walked down the hall to the bedroom, and Charlene went back into the bathroom again, leaving me to sit around and size things up a bit more.

Dad came out in a rush and said he was sorry for having to run off after me only just getting there. I told him I understood. He said he was sorry that I couldn't come too. He told me I should be able to find some grub in the fridge. When they were going out the door he looked at me and said, "Glad you still think about your old man."

So now I'm here in the apartment writing this letter. Good thing I brought some writing paper of my own. No chance of finding any here.

I'm still hungry. I found some bread and made some toast and had a cup of coffee with it. But that was about all I came across in the house that I was willing to face. Oh yeah, and one of those small cans of fruit cocktail. What was in the fridge was a lost cause — left over and dried out. They must eat out a lot, if you can go by all the plastic forks and packs of salt I see lying around.

That's not all that's lying around. A roach in an ashtray. Rolling papers. I'm sure they must smoke up. Not that I care. I guess I'm a bit surprised at the old man doing it, that's all.

Know something? Basement apartments give me the creeps. I don't know why he'd want to live here. One thing for sure, Mom'd never be able to put up with it. That's something that used to bug the old man — the way everything back home had to be so tidy all the time. All the same, I can't see him getting off on this place.

Anyway, it's getting late, and I'm really tired, and I've gone a little crazy writing down so much. Man, this letter is going to weigh a ton. I hope it don't sound like I was running off at the mouth. If it does, sorry about that. I didn't make any of it up. That's just the way it happened.

I'm going to stretch out on the couch now and take a nap until they get back.

I don't want to end this off sounding like I'm sorry for coming. I'm not. It's great to see the old man. I didn't know what to expect, and now I know. That's all. I'll get it straight after a while.

Take it easy,
Terry

P.S. It's the next day. (I know this letter is a pretty gross size like it is, but I want to add on this part. Now I got to make out a new envelope.)

I heard them when they got home last night. You couldn't help but hear them. They were both laughing outside the apartment door. It woke me up, but I pretended I was still asleep. Charlene sounded real crazy — she was laughing about something and couldn't stop. They came inside and everything was quiet for a while.

She went down the hall to the bedroom, and he walked over to the couch and stood up by me. He stayed there for the longest time. I didn't move. Then he went away and came back with a blanket and threw it over me. After a while he turned out the light and walked down the hall. I could hear the door to the bedroom close. Charlene started laughing again. I couldn't get back to sleep for a long time.

Dear Bruce Springsteen,

I'm writing this in the bus station. It'll be another hour before the right bus gets here. It seems like I spend half my time these days waiting for buses.

Myself and Dad have had a good couple of days together. I'm not sorry about leaving, but I am sorry it had to end the way it did. I just packed up and left when he wasn't around. I wish I'd had the nerve to say good-bye to him face to face. But I didn't because I knew that she would probably be around. So here I am at the bus station. (I did leave a note. It wasn't much of one.)

We never really got a chance to talk much. Alone, I mean. The best of it was the couple of hours I spent with him in the club yesterday afternoon, listening to the band practice. The manager let me stay as long as I promised to keep out of sight. He put me in a dark corner near the door to a back room.

The old man finally got what he wanted — the chance to make a living playing in a rock band. I haven't seen him this happy in a long time. They don't play nothing real heavy. They're right into old-time rock and roll — Creedence, Chuck Berry, old Kinks. You should hear them break loose on "I

Fought the Law." They got themselves called Backstreets. Sound familiar? They play a lot of your stuff, too, what they can handle, mostly the newer songs. They do a half-decent job, too. The guy that plays keyboard doubles as a sax player. He's no Clarence, but then again, who is? And they got a few of their own tunes. I doubt if they're anything people would buy on a record, but like the old man said, "It's a start." It sounds like he's got big plans.

Him and two more of the guys from the band sat around at the table where I was while they were taking a break. Dad slipped me what he had left of his beer and bought another one for himself. I never asked for it, and I felt kind of out of place drinking it, but nobody seemed to notice. The guys from the band were joking around about girls and partying and stuff, and they asked me some things about myself. Both of them are younger than the old man, and neither one of them is married. I guess they're out for a good time.

I hope the band sticks together. The old man used to talk a lot about bands he was in years ago and how good they would have been if they'd stuck together. I can see that he's really counting on it this time. I hope it works out for him. They seem like a pretty decent bunch of guys. None of them are tied up with other jobs, and it seems like they're trying to put a lot into it. Like the old man says, they've only been together for five months, but already they're starting to make a name for themselves. And they can only get better. I hope he's right. Wouldn't that be something if they did make it really big? By then I'd be older and I could maybe go on the road with them. Maybe even play with them, who knows?

When they were playing, I really got itchy to be up there onstage. I know I couldn't handle it, not yet anyway. But I also know that's what I want to be doing someday. Like the old man says, you never know how good you can be till you set your mind to it. Coming from the old man, that's really saying something.

That afternoon was the best part of the whole visit. If I could have done that every day, I would have stayed. But I knew the manager didn't think much of me being around there, and besides, after tonight the band is going to be playing out of town for a while. Dad would have let me stay in the apartment if I wanted to, but I couldn't see doing that, not with Charlene there. I can't understand what the old man sees in her.

I won't get into that. Let's just say that after thinking about what choices I got, I'd rather be home. Mom is probably going to have a hell of a lot to say to me for running off like I did, but I'll deal with that when I come to it. I only wish

An hour later . . . I got cut off. I'm finishing the rest of this on the bus. It'll have to be during the stops. It's really hard to write when the bus is moving.

Dad showed up in the bus station. He came in, wearing that same baseball cap, and looked all around. Then he strolled over and sat down next to me. Neither one of us knew what to say. I finally said that I thought it was time that I was going back.

"Now, nobody asked you to go. As far as I'm concerned, you can stay as long as you like," he said.

"I know."

There were people all around us, so I took my backpack and we went outside. We walked along, not saying a word to each other till we came to the end of the building. There was no use in going any farther. I wasn't going back with him.

"It's too bad we didn't have more time together," he said.

"Yeah."

"Man, if I'd known you were coming, I could have planned it better. You got me at a rotten time. I couldn't cancel the trip to Leamington."

"I know that."

"There's a few things I never got around to saying to you."

I glanced at him, but it was easier on the both of us to look somewhere else.

"Man, it's hard to know how to put it," he said.

"You're not coming back."

He couldn't bring himself to say it. I looked at him, and he half shrugged.

"You don't know?" I said.

"Yeah, I know. It just don't sound right, in a way."

"Right? For who?"

"You, I guess."

"Don't worry about me."

"Your mother says you're having a hard time."

"I can handle it."

"Things can't work out between me and your mother, you got to realize that. We want different things. And she's fine. She's happier, if anything. And Amanda — I don't think it bothers her so much."

"You're happy living like you are?"

"I'm no good being tied down."

"You should have thought of that before you got married."

"We all make mistakes."

"I know. Look at me. Your mistake number one."

That really got to him. I'm glad it did.

"Terry. Man, that's not true."

"How come you never write or phone me? One lousy time, that's all." I started to cry then. Man, I couldn't help it.

"I figured it'd be better that way. You can't be hanging on to the past if you're trying to make a new life. You or me. You know me and letters, anyway."

"You could try. You can't just forget about me."

"I think about you every single day."

"Sure you do."

"It's true."

"How can you expect me to believe that?"

He put his arm around my shoulders. "I'll try to do better. That's a promise, man. I will."

I tried to look him in the eyes to see if he really meant it. I wish the hell I hadn't been crying.

"I promise, really. I'll write or something as often as I can."

He let me go. After that we both kept quiet for a long while. At least, it seemed like a long while.

"Know something?" I said finally.

"What?"

"I'm having that cap." And I grabbed the baseball cap off his head and put it in the back pocket of my jeans.

"Hey man, that's my favorite cap."

"I know. I'll send you another one. I promise."

Then we both sort of smiled about it.

"That band you're in," I said to him later, just before I got aboard the bus, "it's half decent, man. You better stick with it."

> That's it,
> Terry

Dear Bruce Springsteen,

Two letters in one day. I'll put them together in the same envelope and save on postage.

Mom hasn't said much to me so far. Dad called her while I was coming home on the bus. That probably had a lot to do with it.

She met me at the station so I wouldn't have to walk. She switched her shift with someone at work to be there.

It *was* a bit tense. I didn't really come out and say it, but I think she got the message that I didn't really run away from her. It was just something I had to do to satisfy my own mind.

While we were driving home Mom started asking me questions about Dad and what he was doing. I told her some things, but I never told her the whole story. Some things are best kept between me and the old man.

I told her a bit about Charlene. I figured that was mostly what she wanted to know, anyway. What I had to say wasn't too good, and that seemed to satisfy her. I didn't lie. Charlene is a bit of a jerk.

Man, I'll tell you one thing. It was good to get home to a half-decent meal. It was even good to see Amanda, believe it or not. For dessert tonight we had homemade lemon pie. Mom knows I really like it. And it's not often that she'll go through all the trouble of making it. I ate over half of the pie myself at supper, and the piece that was left over I got in front of me now, almost gone.

I called up Sean awhile ago. He acted like I'd been gone for a month. He wanted to know everything that happened. I told him I'd see him tomorrow and we'd talk about it. Especially the bit about the band, he should really get off on that.

Right now all I want to do is stretch out on the bed and spend some time trying to get a few things straight.

I'm sure now I did the right thing, taking off like that. I sort of got to see better how different the two of them are. I guess I'm somewhere in the middle. No one could ever make up their mind which one of them I looked like, and I can't really tell which one of them I'm like in other ways. I figured I knew when I left, but now I'm not so sure. In some ways I ended up more mixed up than I was before. But I did what I set out to do. I got to see the old man. I just hope he keeps up his end of the bargain.

Know something else I've been thinking about? You and what you said about your father — how you never could seem to get along with him when you were younger and how you needed to get away, but now you can understand him better and what he was going through. Maybe Dad is something the same way. Maybe he wanted to give me something he never had. Probably he figured we both were better off away from each other. Who knows? I wonder what his old man was like to him when he was growing up. That's something we never ever talked about.

The song I've been playing a lot since I got back is "My Hometown." I've been playing it over and over.

I know you must figure I'm fried out of my skull sometimes, the way I've been firing off these letters to you. Or maybe I should say, if you ever get around to reading them, then maybe you'll think I'm fried. I'm not. And your music's got to be some of the reasons for that. I mean that.

Now I can go to bed. Maybe for a change I'll get a good sleep out of it.

Good night,
Terry

P.S. I never knew this bed could be so comfortable.

Dear Bruce Springsteen,

It's been three days now since I got back home. I'm not sorry yet about coming back. I've been on the go too much to think much about it. Mom dropped a few hints that there's things around the house that I could be doing. Somehow I get the feeling she's trying to keep me busy so I won't have time to think about myself. So far it's probably working. I figure she's testing me, too. I don't know exactly what I mean by that, but it's like she needs to know for sure if I really want to be here.

She got me painting the living room. I'm sort of getting off on it, actually. Makes me feel useful. And it's a good excuse to blast some music. I tell her music keeps me from getting bored. Ever try painting to "Blinded by the Light"? Man, it really does a lot for your stroke.

I've been over at Sean's a fair bit, too. We had some catching up to do. I've started back at the weights. The first time back at them I was a bit stiff, but now it's okay. No muscle city yet, but I looked at myself in the mirror tonight and I can see a big difference. I can. Really.

I told Sean about a lot of what happened on the trip, like the hitchhiking and trying to find the old man and, of course, about the band. He seemed to get off on that, especially when I got into the songs they played and stuff. The way he was talking, he hasn't given up on the idea that someday we could start up one ourselves.

And get this — Sean says the word about this lip-sync concert is spreading like mad. He says almost everyone knows about it, and already loads of girls have been stopping him on the street and calling him up to tell him that they want to get in on it. He started naming them all off, real excited. He figures we're going to have to hold auditions.

That's wicked. We can't do much before school starts. But that's only two weeks away. Man, two weeks. I can't believe it. In one way I hate even thinking about it. Like the homework — that I can do without. In another way, like being able to get this concert thing off the ground, I can't wait for school to start.

I figure I better make the most of these two weeks. You know me — booze parties, wild women, the usual stuff.

Keep it cool,
Terry

Dear Bruce Springsteen,

Aren't some girls just too much? They ignore you for most of your life. Then all of a sudden they start calling you up and making it sound like they've always liked you only you never knew it. What's going on? I don't get it. When I went away it was like I had an unlisted number. I come back, and now the phone is ringing itself off the wall. I can't handle this.

See, the word is out about this concert, and all of a sudden it's got to be the big thing that they all want to get in on. Man, everybody wants to be a rock star. They want to know details, and I can't give them details. I don't even know for sure if it's going ahead. I tell them they'll just have to wait till school starts. "Can I do Madonna?" I got six calls from Madonnas, three from Cyndi Laupers. Heart, the Pointer Sisters — you name it. Guys are starting to phone me now. The Stones, ZZ Top, AC/DC. Kiss, even. I can't handle it. And three calls to do you. I told them you're already booked. I'm starting to leave the phone off the hook.

When I saw Sean yesterday I told him we got to do something about this. They'll drive us off our heads. He said, "Don't knock it, man." He's been getting right off on it, all these different females calling him up. I had to laugh.

We'll just have to wait it out. Kirkland is gone to Disney World with his wife and kids and won't be back till school opens. The only plans we can make now are things like how long the concert should be and the price of the tickets and all that. The real work is going to have to wait till we know for sure we got a place to put it together.

It's starting to get me buzzing. And worried now, too, because people are expecting a lot. What if it bombs? I'll look like a fool. Of course, what I should be doing is thinking the other way. What if it goes over really big? Whatever happens, I'm the one who'll be getting the attention.

I talked it over a bit with Mom. I had to. I had to explain what all the phone calls were about. It really blew her mind that I'd even try something like this, especially when I told her where the money would be going. She don't know me as well as she thinks she does. Anyway, what she said was, I shouldn't be worrying about myself. It's the people we're doing it for that I should be thinking about. Bob Geldof, when he was doing Live Aid, he wasn't worried what anybody thought of him. All he wanted was for people to donate money.

I got to keep that straight in my head. Then I remembered about you, too, and the way you give money away to charities at every concert. I don't think you go around worried about what people think of you. You just get on with the music.

Otherwise you can get really screwed up. At least, that's the way I got it figured.

Right? Right.
Terry

Dear Bruce Springsteen,

I got a letter from the old man. It's not very long, but that's no big deal. He stuck to his word.

He started off with the usual stuff — how are you and hope you had a good trip back and all that kind of thing. Then for the rest of the letter he talked about the band. He knew I'd get off on that, and I guess maybe he couldn't think of much else to write about.

He said the band is doing great. They went over big in Leamington, and the manager of the club wants them back for a full week in October. Right now they're still playing mostly at the club where I was that day. But he says they're starting to get more and more offers to play out of town. Their name is getting around. That's what they plan to do, he says — build up a name for themselves by playing in as many different places as they can.

He didn't say much besides that, but it was real good to get his letter. Now I've got to write him back. Man, you'd think with all the practice I get writing you, I'd have no problem. I figured the same thing till I started. I just couldn't think of the right things to say. I didn't want to talk much about Mom and Amanda because I figured he'd think all I was doing was trying to make him feel guilty. And I didn't want to talk about anything very personal, like how I was feeling now about him and all that. What I ended up talking about for most of the letter was the plans for the concert. Then I mentioned a few things that's been going on around town that I thought he might like to know and that was it. Except what I did was buy a baseball cap (I found one that said "Rock On") and sent it with the letter.

I sent it to him today.

I hear you're playing Toronto tonight. In fact, you're driving them wild just as I'm writing this letter. Wish I could be there. If I think too much about what I'm missing, it could freak me.

School starts next week. If this concert we got planned goes ahead, I'm going to be freaking anyway. Imagine me up onstage in front of hundreds of people. For you, 50,000 is nothing. For me 500 might be like a choke job, man.

Gulp,
Terry

Dear Bruce Springsteen,

The first day of school is tomorrow. Summer is over, except for the weather.

Me and Mom are getting along better than we have for a long while. It seems to be easier now to talk about certain stuff.

Like Nick. I'm the one who brought it up. That's a switch, right? I figured I might as well. I knew it would have to be done sooner or later.

Tonight after Amanda took off to bed and I wasn't doing much except watching something dumb on TV, I asked her why he hadn't been coming around the house.

She looked up from the magazine she was reading, then looked down again before she said anything. "He's not very comfortable here."

"I don't mind if he comes around."

"I'll tell him that."

That's all she was going to say. Probably she figured she'd better not press her luck. Or maybe she didn't believe me.

"I don't mind, really," I said. "I mean, it's your life, right?"

I don't think she knew what to say. All she said was "Okay."
She was playing it real safe.

After five minutes went by (time enough that I figured she
had it out of her mind), she suddenly said, "Perhaps I'll invite
him over to dinner on Sunday if he's not busy."

"Sure, suit yourself."

"He's really nice, you know."

"Are you two getting married?"

She took a while to answer. "Not if it's going to break up
the family."

Dumb as it might sound, that was the first time it dawned
on me how worried she was that if she married the guy, then
I might take off and try to live with the old man. She knew
that if I really wanted to go, I would. I did it once.

"You like him enough to get married to him?"

She didn't come right out and say it, but the way she looked
at me, I could tell what the answer was. I guess it says a lot if
she's willing to put me first. I never thought of it like that
before.

I know I should have said something to her right then. But
I knew that if I did, I'd get embarrassed. I thought she would
have figured out before now that I didn't have such a great
time at the old man's place and that I couldn't see myself
staying there, especially with Charlene around. And it don't
look like the old man's got any plans to break up with her.

When I was getting up to go to my room, I said, "Don't let
me stop you."

I guess we both want to spend some time thinking about it.

What do you say? Think I did the right thing by making it
easier for her? I guess I should be able to figure that one out
for myself. It's just that it's hard to think about there being a
man in the house all the time that's not Dad. Maybe I could
get to like him. As a person, not as a father. Maybe I'll give it
a shot. I guess I should be able to do that much for her.

I made up my mind anyway that it's stupid to worry about things. Man, I spend half my time doing that, worrying about stuff that most of the time I haven't got a hope in hell of changing anyway. Now I'm going to take it one day at a time. And try to think about what I have more than what I don't.

Sounds good to me,
Terry

Dear Bruce Springsteen,

All systems are go for the concert. Kirkland is still behind us all the way. He set up a meeting for us with the principal, and we got permission to use the school auditorium for practice and for the concert. In fact, the principal was really sold on the whole idea. Said it showed a lot of "initiative" on our part.

Sounds good to me.

So the next big step is the auditions. That's the only way we can do it — auditions for everybody, except us. I figure since we're doing most of the work, we should at least get to perform. Nobody's said anything about it. If they do, I'll just tell them where they can get off.

The auditions are set for this Saturday afternoon. There's over twenty acts signed up so far. It's going to be a long day.

Since school started, guess who's been coming around and talking to me all the time? Kristy. I'll never understand girls. I figured I screwed up so bad last time that she'd probably never speak to me again. Now I can't figure out if she really likes me or if she's just doing it to get on my good side because of the concert. Her and some of her friends want to do Heart.

I've been trying to keep away from her because we got to be fair about all this. We can't start playing favorites.

I was never sure anyway how much I liked her. She picked me and worked it around till I asked her out. I'd like to be the one doing the picking for a change.

And there's someone else really worth checking out. Her name's Joanne. I might have mentioned her before. I haven't actually talked to her yet, but I can tell just by looking at her that I like her a lot. I've been doing that quite a bit lately — looking at a bunch of girls and picking out which one I'd want to go out with if I had the chance. Joanne is the kind of girl I really like. She's not the least bit stuck up. That's something I can't handle. And I bet she don't act nice to people in front of their face and then say stuff about them behind their back.

I'm trying to talk myself into calling her up. Man, it's not easy getting up the nerve to make a fool of yourself. I should know.

It might sound like an excuse not to phone her, but I've had a lot of other things on my mind. Nick, for one. He was over tonight for supper. He showed up right at five-thirty like Mom said he would, carrying a bottle of wine. I couldn't picture Dad doing something like that. Wine is not his style. A six-pack of beer, maybe.

I kept doing that all the time he was in the house — comparing him to the old man. I know it wasn't fair, but I couldn't help it. I managed to be a bit more civilized than the last time he was here. I tried to carry on a conversation with him, at least. I still wasn't being myself, though, and I'm sure Mom could tell.

So what do I think of him now? He's okay. I'm not sure I could handle him living with us. He's real good to Mom — like, he helped her with the dishes after the meal, something the old man would never do. Then again, maybe he was just doing that to get on our good side. It's hard to tell.

I know that's not being very fair to Mom, to think that she'd get married to someone who wouldn't treat us right. I just don't know him enough to make up my mind what to think.

All that might change. He's asked me if I want to go canoe-ing with him next Sunday. I haven't made up my mind.

More decisions,
Terry

Dear Bruce Springsteen,

Me and Sean got together today to figure out what we're going to do in the concert. All along we knew it was going to be one of your songs. Today we decided what one.

This is embarrassing. I almost had my mind made up not to say anything about what we're doing. Man, I know you think a lot about your music, and you wouldn't want some jerks up there making a fool of one of your songs. Just try to remember, it's for a good cause.

We finally decided on "Dancing in the Dark," for a lot of different reasons. We wanted something everybody knew and one where we could act out the video. We needed something that wasn't too long and had a beat that the audience could move to. Plus, I really get off on the part in the video where you pull up the girl from the audience and start to dance with her.

I'm going to be doing you, and Sean'll be Nils. He made me promise him he could be out front a lot. We've got this big guy who said he'll do Clarence, and another dude on drums and one on keyboard. The audience'll have to use their imagination for the other guys.

No matter how many are there, most of the attention is going to be on me. Now I'm really starting to worry about whether or not I can pull it off. I mean, that's asking a lot of someone like me. The last time I got up in front of a crowd was to play one of the seven dwarfs in second grade. What I'm counting on is that once I get into the music, I'll forget all about being nervous. I've practiced enough, that's for sure. I guess I'll make a fool of myself if I got to. I don't care.

That don't sound so good, does it? I'm still not sure I should have mentioned anything much about this. If it don't come off, I might be sorry I ever tried it. And believe me, man, nobody'll ever know, except us and 500 other people. Think about it this way—if I make a fool of myself or of you, it's not because I want to.

Forget I said that.
Terry

Dear Bruce Springsteen,

It was a long afternoon yesterday—four hours of auditions for an hour show. It was mad. I never want to hear Madonna's voice again. And I'm sure Kirkland don't either. The same song four different times, no kidding. And each girl who did it was a little wilder than the one before.

We had twenty-four acts show up. Our job was to cut that down to eight. With the two others, that'll make ten. We talked about it a lot, and like Kirkland said, any more and the whole thing is going to start to lose its edge.

We stayed behind after everybody else was gone and made our decisions. For some of the acts it was no sweat at all—everybody agreed they had to go in. Like the guys who did ZZ Top. They were great, you know, with the long beards and the dance steps together. And there were four guys who did the Beatles, like in the old clips you see of them with the suits that matched and the mop haircuts, singing "I Wanna Hold Your Hand." Xerox all the way. Something else that really knocked us over was these girls who did a mad, mad job on "Girls Just Wanna Have Fun." They were spot-on.

It was harder making up our minds when there were like two or more of the same act with not much difference between them. Sean said he didn't care too much which one of them got it, especially when it was girls and we had to face them on Monday. We mostly let Kirkland persuade us one way or the other. That way we could say it was him who made the final decision.

Anyway, we got ten solid acts, including us, and Kirkland doing a take-off on Michael Jackson. (It's real crazy. I've seen him do bits of it in guitar class.) Now comes practice, and more practice. We're not going ahead with it till it's first rate.

That's where the concert stands now. I'll keep you posted. I'm sure you'll be holding your breath.

I mentioned before about Nick asking me to go canoeing with him. It was on my mind all week whether or not I should go. Mom never said nothing to me one way or the other. It was all my own decision.

When he phoned Thursday night I still hadn't made up my mind. I ended up saying yes because I'm never very good at saying no to people when they really want me to do something. I can never think of an excuse that don't sound like I'm lying.

He came and picked me up this morning, and we went across Ailsa Lake. It was the first time I'd ever been in a canoe. Nick knows a lot about how to handle one.

The trip turned out better than I figured it would. Both of us were on edge a bit, and he seemed to be talking a lot. But he didn't try to load me up with crap. It was okay.

I found out a lot about him that I never knew before. Where he works and stuff. He's got a good job. He's assistant manager in one of the banks. Sounds pretty boring to me, but he says he likes it, for now. Says he wants to start up his own business one of these days. He's got lots of plans by the way he was talking.

Like I said, it was okay. I'd probably go out again.

Talk to you later,
Terry

P.S. Man, how do you make dancing onstage like that look so easy?

Dear Bruce Springsteen,

I been in a rotten mood for the past couple of days. I guess it shows.

It's got nothing to do with the concert. That's pretty much in shape. The time is all set — Friday afternoon, October 4. At first we figured maybe we'd have to have it at night because we wouldn't get the time off from school. But the principal said we could have two school periods Friday afternoon. I guess Kirkland did some talking. Although from what he said, the principal is still behind us all the way.

So it's not the concert. I guess part of it is the fact that I still haven't phoned Joanne. I really want to, but I'm chicken. Man, I'm really scared of screwing it up. I like her too much to take a chance on it.

It's nuts. I haven't said ten words to the girl in my life, and I see her every day in school. I'm always wondering what she thinks of me. Of course she probably don't think about me, period. She's not one of the ones who came around when all this about the concert started. And she wasn't one of the people that auditioned. Thank God.

Kristy was, and she didn't make it. Now she don't talk to me anymore. That's okay by me. I never really liked her that much anyway.

You have lots of experience with girls. What would you do? Probably you'd write a song about it.

And something else, too.

I haven't heard from the old man for over three weeks now. It's got me wondering if he really meant what he said.

So long,
Terry

September 20

Dear Bruce Springsteen,

Nick is not such a jerk as I thought he was. He's okay, in his own way. He comes over to the apartment a lot now. I don't mind it so much.

I haven't gone canoeing with him a second time, even though I said I would. He's been after me to go duck hunting this weekend. I don't think I will. It's something I never did with the old man, even though we planned on it a few times. It never worked out that we could go.

I still haven't heard back from him — the old man, I mean. It'll be four weeks Monday. If he's on the road a lot, probably he hasn't got time to write or call. It's really starting to bug me, though. There's no use saying it's not.

And I still haven't called Joanne.

This is going to be a short letter. I mightn't even mail it. It's hardly worth wasting a stamp on.

I just had to do something with my time.

Terry

Dear Bruce Springsteen,

Happy Birthday! I hope, if you made a wish, it comes true. Mine did. A letter came from the old man. I figured it would. Two pages long. They've been on the road for a couple of weeks, and he said he didn't have much of a chance to write. He says they got solid bookings till after Christmas, and he says it looks real good for the new year. He sounds real excited about all this. Can't blame him. I would be, too.

He talked a lot about the band. A lot about some of the new songs they've been working on. He said he got a real kick out of the cap I sent. He wears it all the time.

He mentioned about the concert and how he's proud of what I'm doing. Said he hopes it works out. Then he said for me not to forget about making my own music, because that's what it's all about.

That got me back to working on the song I've been writing for Joanne. Except now it's about a lot of different stuff. I nearly got it finished. Some of the words aren't the way I want them yet and the music needs a lot of work, but it's better than the other one. It's more me.

It's not long now before the concert — a week and a half. The lineup is all set. We've been having practice every day after school. We've worked out some of the problems, like changing the set between acts. The backstage area is not very big, so we got to keep things down to just the basic stuff. It's hard. Some of them wanted a load of props for their one song. Besides, we haven't got the time between songs to be hauling things away and bringing more stuff in. We managed to get our hands on a drum set that we can set up and leave in one spot for the whole show.

And what we're doing is making one backdrop for everyone — black with neon paint running through it, like thunderbolts. And we're setting up a couple of strobes and some colored spotlights for whoever wants to use them. We got all kinds of volunteers who want to get in on what's happening, so we put two people in charge of the lights, someone else on curtains, and a couple of others to take care of the props.

Man, it's a lot of headaches, but I can see it coming together. It should be good for a laugh if nothing else.

By the way, I did go out duck hunting with Nick after all. Had a half-decent time. We didn't get any ducks, but it was all right just to be out like that away from everything. I'll tell you about it sometime. Right now I got to get some sleep. And I got to think about what I'm going to say to the old man when I write him back.

Still haven't phoned Joanne.

What else is new?
Terry

Dear Bruce Springsteen,

I made up my mind. I told Mom if she wants to marry him that's fine by me, just don't expect miracles.

When she never said nothing it got me thinking that she really does want to marry him. That all she's waiting for is the divorce to come through. Then I started wondering if we're going to be moving from this apartment and whether or not that's going to screw things up even more. (I'm still a great one for thinking ahead.) I'm sorry now that I said anything to her.

Still, it's the only way. What other choice have I got? I told the old man that on the letter.

The hell with it, I say. In a few years I'll be old enough that I can go where I want and do what I want.

All that's on my mind. Plus the concert. That's in two days. One last run-through tomorrow and then we'll be as ready as we're ever going to be. I think it's looking pretty good, but maybe it'll go over like a wet rag. Who knows?

I haven't had time for anything else. I know, I know, I should be making a play for Joanne, but I'm not. I'm too tied up with other things right now, and I still haven't got the guts to do it. Man, I'll probably be old and gray and still just as dumb when it comes to girls.

I'm a real one for looking on the bright side, right?

Tell you what, though. It helps to know that you weren't exactly Casanova when you were my age.

I did send her a note—with no name signed to it. It said to make sure she sat up front during the concert.

I'm going to try carrying around that baseball cap that I took from the old man when I'm on during the concert—in the back pocket of my jeans. It might work for me, too.

I'm hyper. I guess it shows. I can't really concentrate, so it's just as well to stop this letter.

If you knew what was happening, you'd be wishing me luck.

Same to you,
Terry

P.S. I almost forgot—tonight is the last night of your tour. Rock 'em silly.

Dear Bruce Springsteen,

Wicked. Wicked. Better than that. Totally mad. Fried! (We raised over a thousand bucks. Some people even threw in extra money at the end.) Man, you wouldn't believe the concert went over so good. And that's not the best part of it. Tell you more about that later.

First I got to talk about the others in the show. Like I said before, I wasn't sure about a lot of things. But right from the first song we had the audience with us, the same as if it was a real concert.

I did the introduction. I started off with a few words thanking people for coming and saying that I hoped everybody would have a good time but that we weren't just doing it for fun. That some of us got it pretty tough and it's up to us to help each other out. I kept it short, but it was important what I said.

Then we let the music rip. The curtain opened and onstage were the guys doing ZZ Top. They were a riot. They really put a lot into it, more even than in practice. It was a perfect way to start off because it really got the audience worked up. By the end of the song most of them were on their feet clapping, some of them dancing to the music. It was better than I ever expected.

Once we got them like that, we knew we had to keep things moving. That's why we really worked our butts off to get one act offstage and the next one on and ready to go before they got restless. It got a bit hairy at times behind stage, but nobody lost their cool.

After ZZ Top, we hit with Cyndi Lauper. The music started, and she came dancing through the middle of the auditorium with a trail of backup singers behind her, all dressed really wild, with hair and makeup all colors. The crowd loved it, especially when this guy came on at the end dressed like a wrestler and carried her offstage.

From that to Bryan Adams (especially for the girls) to AC/DC (for the beer party crowd). Then the Stones (a guy in tenth grade did a wicked Mick Jagger).

After that, Tina Turner. Hot! Hot! This girl Lynda, who is really built and don't mind showing it, left the guys with their tongues hanging out after that one.

Then Kirkland came on and sang his version of "Billy Jean," only he had the words all changed. He came out with the hair greased, the dance moves, the whole bit. Except after a while he started stumbling and tripping himself up. The place was roaring.

A tough act to follow, but the three girls who came on as the Pointer Sisters did a really decent job. They could have been a bit looser at the beginning, but they picked it up after a while and really got things moving. Enough to get us into the last two acts. We'd kept the Beatles until the second last. They were just as big a hit as we'd counted on. Perfect, right out of the sixties. A good change of pace for the finale — us.

And we were mean! We were the killer of the show. No need to worry, man — I did you good.

By the time it was our turn, I was so wound up in the

show, I wasn't the least bit nervous. I could have faced a crowd ten times the size and not batted an eye — till the curtain opened.

Then it hit me. For half a second it was panic city, till that drumbeat started driving itself through me, and I let loose in the hips and with the shoulders. And got the fingers snapping.

The first couple of words caught me off guard, but after that I was right into it all the way — the mouth working just as hard as if I was really singing, the arms whipping through the air, looks flashing around the audience. Dancing around the stage, even playing off against Sean on guitar. Wicked. I loved it. Sean, too, especially when he saw all these girls cheering us on.

Once they got over the shock of seeing me up there, the crowd started yelling and whistling, and some of them even started singing out the words. It was like I was meant to be there.

Every now and then I'd glance around the front rows at the girls, because I knew what they were thinking. Who's he going to get to dance with him onstage at the end of the song? I knew who it was and I knew right where she was sitting. She must have got the note.

And when the last words came — "Hey baby" — and I tossed the microphone over my shoulder to Sean, I didn't hesitate one bit. I looked right at Joanne and waved her up onstage. She was a little out of it, but she came right away, running the last part up the steps, so the two of us could dance together with the sax blaring and the crowd cheering us on. Thanks, man, thanks for putting in that bit in the video. You might have really started something between us.

And when it was over and she went back to her seat, the cheering went on and on. Even backstage with the curtain closed, they were out there shouting "More! More!" like there just had to be another song we could do.

We hadn't practiced anything else. What could we do? We were looking around, desperate. We went outside the curtain and took another bow. The crowd was on their feet, crazy for more.

Backstage again, and we decided we'd just have to pack it in. We weren't going to take a chance on messing up a song we never practiced. After a while the cheering died away.

But it was wicked while it lasted.

And I'm smiling too, now.
Terry

Dear Bruce Springsteen,

I read in the paper that during that last show in L.A. on Wednesday you brought your wife onstage and gave her a real long kiss. Nice work. I can't compete with that. Not yet. But I'm pretty sure me and Joanne got something going.

I phoned her today after I finally came down from the concert. Man, I was flying so high it took me that long to get back to earth.

I didn't know what to expect, but I knew I had to call her. Maybe I had embarrassed her, and maybe she wouldn't want anything to do with me. Maybe she was sorry she ever went up on that stage. I had to phone her, though. I couldn't wait till I went back to school, not with all those people around.

She answered the phone. I thought for a second that I was really going to choke up. But after the first minute it was great.

We talked for over an hour. Do you believe it? No cotton-balls, no notes, nothing. We talked about the concert, of course, but then about all kinds of other stuff. She loves your music. Her favorite album is *The River*.

And we made a date. Man, when I got off the phone I was back up in the clouds again. Something's hit me and I'm going around like I'm on dope.

I can't write any more. I'm really out of it.

Wicked,
Terry

Dear Bruce Springsteen,

It's official. They're getting married. No big surprise. And you know something? It don't really bother me much. It's not like I couldn't see it coming.

We were all sitting down at the supper table — the four of us — when Mom told Amanda and me. Amanda got all excited and wanted to know if she could be one of the bridesmaids and get a new dress and carry a bouquet. That's Amanda for you.

Mom said it wasn't going to be that kind of wedding. Just something simple.

I didn't really say much. I said congratulations in a nice sort of way that sounded like I meant it. That was enough. I guess they were relieved.

They didn't really get into any details, which was okay, because I didn't really want to talk about it. You know the way I am. I need time for things to sink in.

Now, after a few days thinking about it, it's okay. At least, I think so. Like I told Mom, I'll do what I can to make it work. They can't expect any more than that.

I wrote Dad and told him how I felt about the whole thing. It wasn't an easy letter to write. I told him I thought it was the best thing for everyone, Mom getting married again. It wouldn't change much between him and me. I still wanted for us to see each other. I laid things out pretty straight — that he was still my father and I expected a lot from him. I didn't fool around. I told him what I was feeling.

It was only a few days ago that I sent the letter. Today I got one back. He must have written it as soon as he got mine.

There was personal stuff in the letter that really got to me, stuff that I wouldn't tell anyone, not even you. I never figured the old man cared that much about me.

Anyway, I'm almost glad in a way that Mom *is* getting married. It means there's more of an excuse to go visit him. In fact, he asked if I want to spend part of Christmas with him. Sounds good to me. He says if he can work it, then maybe we could go off somewhere next summer camping or something, just the two of us. I really hope he means that.

I unloaded a lot of this on Joanne when we were out together tonight. I figured I might as well. She should know what she's in for if she's going out with me. Guess what she said? Don't let it get to me. Think positive. And then she hugged into me. I can handle that.

I'm pretty positive I like her a lot and that she likes me. Me and Joanne and Sean's new girl friend are all going over to Sean's place Friday night. We're renting a couple of movies and cooking up pizza. Should be good.

I better go. There's something I forgot to tell Joanne, and I got to call her back before she goes to bed. Man, it's a tough life being such a lady-killer.

Oh yeah, I almost forgot. The Smiths were really pleased about the money. They told me what they're going to spend it on — bedroom furniture and clothes for the kids. And the rest they're going to put away for Christmas. They asked me if I'd come over and baby-sit sometime. I said sure.

Talk to you later,
Terry

Dear Bruce Springsteen,

It's been a long time since I wrote you. I've thought about it a lot, and I think maybe I'll make this the last one.

When I started all this I really needed someone I could talk to. (Lucky you, right?) Now I'm going to give you a break and shut up.

The past few months have been a bit crazy. The letters that I wrote to you are the one thing that tied it all together.

Sometimes I wonder if you ever read any of the letters. Maybe now that your tour is over, you might get around to it. Like I said before, it wouldn't really bother me if I knew you didn't. I kind of like to think you did, but I know you still got a lot of things to be doing. Maybe someday I'll hear from you. Who knows?

I read once that after a concert some guy you never met before started talking to you and asked you to his house for a meal with his family. And you said yes. Man, that offer goes for me, too. Mom could cook up her famous spaghetti. Of course I'd have to call up the old man and get him to make a special trip here. We'd have a lot to talk about. That's an open invitation, if you're ever in this part of the country.

Maybe you'll come closer to where I live on your next tour. You've got a lot of fans around here. If you do, I'll be the first one to buy tickets.

But no matter if you come near here or not, I'll still be going to see you. That's the one promise I made to myself — to see you in concert the next time you're on tour. I'll be the one in the front row looking like he's in heaven.

My time for writing letters will be taken up with writing to the old man, I hope. I owe him one now. It's me that's being the slacker this time.

Well, I guess this is the end of the line, Bruce Springsteen, man. (I was going to call you just Bruce for once, but I couldn't bring myself to do it.) Anyway, this is about it.

Remember — take it easy. Take a break, you've been touring for a long time. Enjoy your life, man, and remember, if you ever have kids, spend lots of time with them.

And keep the music coming. I'll be watching out for a new album.

Yours truly, man,
Terry Blanchard